A
DRINK
WITH
DEATH

Where's Death Series

Book 1

By S. G. Blinn

This interactive historical fiction takes you deep into the world of the 1920s Prohibition. As the government tries to control the trade and consumption of alcohol, a leader rises and brings a community together to fight back.

But, hiding amongst the chaos is Death, who is disguised as one of their own. One character doesn't belong, one person isn't who they claim to be.

Can you find Death before the world burns?

A Drink With Death

This is a work of fiction. Any resemblance to places, events, or real people are entirely coincidental.

© 2022 S. G. Blinn

ISBN: 978-0-578-35011-0

Printed in the United States of America

Visit my website at: **www.sgblinn.com**

Dedicated to:

Those who seek freedom in a book.

May every page bring you happiness, adventure, and a tissue
box full of emotions.

Dear Reader,

Greetings.

I am **Death**.

My time is everlasting, and sometimes, watching can become a tad boring. So, I have decided to take on a human form and see what the hype of being alive is all about. My time will be short because my role is set, but that does not mean I cannot have a little fun.

Let us play a game between the two of us.

I will not tell you who I created to be my vessel, but I want you to guess who I could be. Do not worry, I will make the narrative fun and exciting, but know I am there, watching, waiting to take the souls from this life into the next.

Can you guess which one I am?

Have fun.

Sincerely,

Death

Suspect List

- <u>Patrick O'Malley:</u> Grocer/ Bootleg Runner
- <u>Gretchen Laird:</u> Secretary
- <u>Conner McDonald:</u> Bootleg Runner
- <u>Finnick O'Malley:</u> Grocer/ Bootleg Runner
- <u>Lawrence Murphy:</u> Unemployed
- <u>Cameron Mitchell:</u> Student
- <u>Sarah Monroe:</u> School Teacher/ Accountant
- <u>Connie Murphy:</u> Waitress
- <u>Manny Laird:</u> Driver
- <u>Porter:</u> Bootlegger Boss
- <u>Betty Tyler:</u> Prostitute
- <u>Vincent Sullivan:</u> Store Clerk
- <u>Linda Bishop:</u> Unemployed
- <u>Paul Daniels:</u> Secretary
- <u>Benjamin Colins:</u> Police Detective
- <u>Hamilton Murphy:</u> Senator
- <u>Special Agent Marcus Willard:</u> Prohis/Prohibition Agent

PROLOGUE

Boston, Massachusetts
Year: 1921

The night was no longer silent. High-pitched screams filled every alley as they reflected the unspeakable horrors that existed within the shadows. You either had to fight or were told to hide; there was no in-between. Blood stained the very ground that once held such promise, but as a hastened group of feet ran up a familiar set of stairs, they carried a large man who obviously was wounded.

"Goddamn it, Finny, this hurts like a son of a bitch!" The man, Patrick, groaned as his brother plopped his bullet-ridden body on the table. Pop. Pop. The sounds of the gunfire in the distance added to the agony that the two men were feeling. Pop. It was all anyone could hear aside from Patrick's complaints about the obvious bullet wounds in his chest.

"That sounds like a complaint," his brother, Finnick, teased.

"It sure doesn't tickle," Patrick said, trying to laugh but flinching at the pain. These two men had the outward appearance of large and barbaric. Dirtied clothing, unkempt personal hygiene, and a mass of red hair that immediately associated them with a certain group of people. A group that was currently fighting for their lives.

"Quiet, or they might hear you," Finnick replied in a hushed tone as he shoved used rags in his brother's mouth.

Even though no one could understand him, Patrick continued to give his commentary. He would rather die with a voice than rot away in silence. It was useless to try to stop him, but the more he spoke, the more Patrick struggled to breathe.

"What can I do?" a woman behind them whispered as Finnick turned.

Sarah. She was as plain as any woman could be, but it was not her voice that spoke. Another woman was at her side, a small, lively character that spoke with an accent of the South. She had the same matched expression of worry that made Finnick displeased.

"I have a stash under the floorboards in the kitchen. Get me something to ease his pain," Finnick began, but Linda, the other woman objected.

"If they find any contraband in this house, you will be shot on sight!" Linda exclaimed.

It was not supposed to end this way. What the brothers did was illegal, but it was easy. All they had to do was take the product from the drop site and deliver it to where they were instructed.

Never once did they open the crates or tell a soul what was in them. What Finnick had under the floorboards were gifts from Porter, the man who ran this city's nightlife. A man who this whole situation was all about.

"Get it now!" Finnick barked as Sarah rushed out of the room.

"Is Porter coming?" Linda asked.

At the mention of the name, a new set of footsteps entered the room. The smell radiating from this new man was identical to the brothers. Sweat, dirt, blood, and gunpowder. They all were fighting as their brothers and sisters were doing this very moment. But rather than be out there, Porter knew he needed to be here with a man that didn't have much time.

"Move aside, Finnick. Let me see what I can do," Porter said as he tore open the remains of Patrick's shirt to get a better look.

Three bullet holes greeted him, and every time Patrick took a breath, blood seeped out. It did not look good, and with the amount of blood loss, Porter knew this young man was not going to see the next sunrise. No matter what was done, there was no saving him.

"I got the whiskey!" Sarah proclaimed as she tripped over her own feet.

Crash. When her body hit the ground, all noise stopped. Golden elixir slowly seeped from the broken glass and disappeared in-between the broken floorboards. Slowly, Sarah stood, but they all focused on that broken glass as if it were a sign from above.

Alcohol was illegal now, and because no one listened, everyone was going to meet the reaper one way or another.

"Listen to me very carefully, Finnick. Patrick will not make it—" Porter began and raised his hand to silence the brother to avoid an argument.

"If you and the girls want to survive the night, you need to make a choice. I never forced you into this life, but I am giving you the opportunity to get out. You need to leave, run as far away from me and this city as possible, and take them with you," Porter said calmly, knowing full well Finnick would refuse.

Everyone was being hunted. All those who opposed the law were no longer given a second chance. It did not matter if you were a man, woman, or child; anyone who dared raise arms against the Prohis, the Prohibition agents, were met with the same brutal end they all were facing this very night.

"I will take care of the body. You can do what you Irish boys do and say your goodbyes, but I need the body…" Porter spoke, but he soon realized Finnick was no longer listening.

"Porter?" Sarah whispered.

"Let's give them time to say goodbye," Porter replied and slowly walked away.

The three of them looked once more at the brothers before they walked into the darkness. There was nothing anyone could do, and with the sounds of gunfire getting closer, they needed to move quickly to avoid being detected.

"It was not supposed to be this way, Pat…You and I were supposed to take on the world once we got enough money," Finnick whispered as he held Patrick's hand.

He would do anything to have his brother live. As he watched Patrick struggle to breathe, he closed his eyes and prayed. These two were not the religious type, they have seen so much damnation to believe in something outside of what they could see, but he prayed anyway. He prayed for a miracle, one where Patrick lived and whoever shot him would burn in hell.

CHAPTER ONE

Three Months Earlier

It was like any other morning in the city of Boston. The moment the sun rose, the clock started to tick on the workable hours of the day. Money. It was what made the world a bigger and better place. Everyone was taught the value of money from the moment they were born. It was the elixir of life.

The community did what it could to survive. Many came to this country to find work and avoid the terror that plagued their homeland. Those who were lucky enough to start a business got the support of the community around them.

One popular Irish-owned-and-run operation was O'Malley's Grocery. A father with his two sons brought the business up from nothing, and now, this is where our story continues…

—

"Good morning, Ms. Laird. How can I help you?" Finnick asked as a woman before him looked away bashfully.

He was a lovely man in looks. Ms. Laird was not the first person to form a little crush on one of the O'Malley brothers, but she, like the rest, knew better than to get too close. An extensive line was forming behind her as the young woman struggled to find the right words to respond to the man before her.

"Hurry it up, sweet thing. We do not have all day!" a man hollered from the end of the line as the bashful woman finally held up a list.

"Leave her alone! Can't you see she is shy?" another man added, coming to Ms. Laird's aid.

Finnick's large, calloused hands looked almost ridiculous against Ms. Laird's gloved fingers. It was the slightest touch that caused the woman to jump out of her heels and scurry away. It was not unusual for Ms. Gretchen Laird to act this way; everyone seemed to know she had a mad crush on Finnick O'Malley, well, almost everyone. Finnick was a large boy but was denser than a bag of rocks.

"If you keep chasing off all the women, I will never have any grandkids," Finnick's father teased.

"I have no idea what you are talking about," Finnick objected.

"Finny," his father responded in a stern tone.

"I am serious!"

"Were you mean?"

"No, sir. Nice as I was taught."

"Were you a gentleman? You know how the ladies always like a gentleman," his father teased, which caused a few customers to giggle.

"I swear, as I always do. I never scared her. I am always a gentleman and very polite. I do not know what that lass's problem is." Finnick started to work on the list he was given.

The grocery store was family-owned and operated. Finnick's father took immense pride in the business and expected his sons to pitch in where help was needed. Today, the store was busy.

They already had four orders to complete, with two people waiting ahead of Ms. Laird. It would be easier for them if there was a third body to help with the crowd, but Patrick was late once again from his delivery, leaving the two men shorthanded.

—

"This is going to be the last time, O'Malley," a man promised as a dust-covered gentleman with a grin from ear-to-ear looked towards him.

"Keep telling yourself that, Senator. Where is the money? Or would you like the entire world to know about you and Vincent Sullivan?" Patrick O'Malley teased, as that shit-eating grin was still evident on his face.

"You speak lies!" the senator snapped.

"So, should I go to Vincent and ask what he thinks about this current argument?" Patrick said as he enjoyed watching the redness increase on the senator's face.

"Watch your goddamn mouth!" the senator barked, but like the good dog he was, he reached into his pocket and withdrew an envelope.

"Good boy." Patrick smiled.

The alleyways between the buildings in the Irish communities were always filled with deals. Either in contraband, women, or money. Today was no different, but when the senator held out the envelope, rather than handing it over willingly, he held it up for Patrick to see.

"This is the last time," the senator sneered.

"I will say when it is the last time," Patrick threatened, rolling up his sleeves.

"I have paid you as requested, and if you want your father's store to stay out of the hands of the local authorities, you will not ask me again," The smug expression left Patrick's face.

"That was the wrong thing to say—" Patrick took giant steps towards him.

There was not much of a height difference between the two men, but the level of wealth was obvious. Patrick O'Malley had patched pants and his button-up shirt had not been washed in days. It did not matter if he stunk or if he hadn't shaved in a week; no one told an O'Malley what to do.

Each step kicked up dirt to further add to the level of dismay that was Patrick O'Malley. When he finally approached the man, he pulled back his arm and balled up his fist. In one quick action, Patrick punched the senator hard in the stomach.

If Patrick hit his face, the impact would have risked a broken bone or bruising skin. That could have been hard for the senator to hide and easy for charges to be pressed. So, that left Patrick with one choice.

"Oomph!" the senator let out as he leaned forward to clutch his stomach.

With ease, Patrick snatched the money from his free hand and leaned over. The man before him was gasping for breath. Maybe Patrick hit him a little too hard, but the deed was done. No matter what they did next, the other would be in trouble, so Patrick leaned down and whispered a sweet song into the senator's ear.

"You listen to me very carefully. I do not care the name of your cologne, how many cars you have, and where your daddy stuck his pecker. If you do not want the world to know about you and Vincent,

I suggest you meet me here next month. Same time, but double the payment for your arrogance and stupidity."

"Patty!" Finnick yelled the moment he opened the back door of the store.

Patrick turned quickly and hid the senator from view of his brother. Finnick didn't care what he was doing, but the attitude made it evident that Patrick was needed inside the store. The store must have been slammed if his brother had an angry expression on his face.

"A man can't catch a break around here?" Patrick responded.

"Get your ass inside!" Finnick hollered and slammed the door.

"Run back to your daddy now, boy—" the senator growled.

"Want to go another round?" Patrick threatened and turned to look at him.

The two men fell silent as the senator stood and carefully straightened himself out. It was bad luck that Patrick O'Malley caught the senator having relations with Vincent Sullivan, a store hand at the clothing business next door. There was nothing more scandalous than relations with someone other than your spouse. Add the same gender to it, and the papers would eat it up. No one cared how he felt about Vincent; all they cared about was a future candidate for the presidency and his personal relations. He couldn't let this get out.

—

The senator played that night repeatedly in his head. The two of them were always so careful but that night, they got caught up in the moment. They had left the cinema, and it was raining. He had wanted to end the night on a good note, but regardless of how he felt then, the repercussions of his actions had been constant ever since.

"Senator Murphy, are you all right?" Gretchen Laird asked.

Gretchen, like everyone else, was cutting through the alleyways to get to where she needed to go. The few groceries she had in her hand showed she had just left O'Malley's Grocery. These passages were less crowded and easier to maneuver. When Senator Murphy turned to look at her, he put on a fake smile, knowing full well he had no true explanation as to what he was doing there.

Image was everything. He needed to act like it was nothing more than a coincidence they met, and if people saw him walking back to City Hall with a woman, any slander Patrick O'Malley might say would have less power, at least for today. The plan was set; all he had to do was make the woman agree to it.

"I'm fine, Ms. Laird. Care to walk with me?" he asked and offered an arm.

It was customary for a woman to be escorted. Gretchen was young and ambitious to go after an Irishman, but as they walked, it seemed she needed to fill the silence with chatter. Senator Murphy hated small talk. It was nothing more than noise with no objective, but he had to endure it, if only for the few moments to get to their destination.

"Are you sure you are all right? There is some dirt on your jacket," Gretchen mentioned and motioned towards his unkempt attire.

"Don't worry yourself with me."

"I apologize for asking, sir, but do you think this new law will work?" she asked as it took Senator Murphy all the willpower he had not to roll his eyes at the woman, but at least she was no longer focusing on him.

"Our world is in crisis, Ms. Laird. Crime is at an all-time high while families are suffering from the influence of alcohol and other illicit activities. This law is a step in the right direction, one that I fully support."

"But the law prohibits drinking."

"Indeed. The Eighteenth Amendment will hold, already we are seeing a decrease in prison numbers, and men are safely returning home to their families."

"It would be nice to help everyone."

"This is the first step. After that, we will be able to help everyone who wants to make a better life for themselves." Senator Murphy looked away from the homeless people around him, trying hard not to show his disgust.

It had only been two months since the Eighteenth Amendment had passed, the ban of alcohol consumption, transportation, and manufacturing. It was what people called "The Nobel Experiment". The senator was in good spirits that individuals would be helped as they were promised, but he knew it was a way of control, one he fully supported.

—

"You seem uncomfortable," a man whispered to the woman walking at his side.

They both looked from Senator Murphy, who was escorting a young woman. The look of annoyance was evident on his face, but the woman didn't seem to notice.

These two new individuals were on the other side of the street, far away from the world of tailored suits and shiny shoes. A world they both so desperately wanted to escape.

"I do not like this idea, Lawrence. I mean, I need the job, but working for Porter is risky," she said as Lawrence grabbed her wrist and pulled her down an alley.

Nothing about their outright appearance made them stand out. Secondhand clothing that was too big and always dirty. They were never noticed, which made Lawrence happy, but happiness was not currently on his face.

There were trash piles at every street corner. Lawrence dragged Connie deeper into the shadows. They needed to speak in private, so she could learn about the mistake she had just made.

"You need to be careful about what you say out in the open, Connie. We are not in the home anymore; this is serious," he said as the woman sighed and leaned her head against his chest.

"I know, Lawrence…I am not stupid," she muttered, unable to look at him in the eye.

Unlike the O'Malley brothers, Lawrence Murphy did not have the social standing as Senator Hamilton Murphy, but he knew how to use his surroundings to his advantage. He could be clean if he wanted, but then he would stand out. When his business got off the ground, Lawrence would no longer have to steal clothing from the beggars or food from O'Malleys. He would make something of himself; all he needed was a break.

"I am scared. This will be my first job, and what they make women wear in those places, I can't do it," Connie whined as Lawrence took her face into his gloved hand and forced her to look at him.

"Listen to me. I have a plan."

"This is serious, Lawrence," she said and that made him angry.

"I am serious! The facilities are in the mountains, only a few hours' drive from here. There is already a crew in place to move the merchandise into the city. I need to know where Porter will not be, so I have no complications."

"Porter owns this city. You cannot walk up to anyone and ask where his next shipment will be."

"That is where you come in." It all clicked for her.

"No," Connie responded.

"Please, Connie, I can't do this without you."

"I said no, Lawrence. I can't do it," she exclaimed, ready to walk away, but he blocked the only exit out of the alley.

"Why can't you do this for me?"

"They will have me in a dress that leaves nothing to the imagination. My hair is always a mess, and no number of preparations will make this hair listen. I will never be able to wear that headgear." She joked.

Connie admired the low, rumbly laugh that came out of him. His thick, tall body matched his laughter, and how his beard seemed to grow over night was magical. He was everything she wanted in a man, but because they grew up together as kids in the home, he would never look at her the same as she did him.

"You will be beautiful no matter what they put you in."

"You are only saying that to make me feel better."

"I am not. Remember, you are not alone in there. I will make one of my boys walk you to and from the block. I will also always have one inside. You will be fine."

"Do you really think I can do this?" Connie asked as the uncertainty in her tone crept up again.

"I know you can. Everyone will love you," Lawrence responded as the woman in his arms laughed.

He always had a way with her, even when they were kids. She would have the common sense to say no to him, but the moment he opened his mouth and spoke those sweet words, she agreed to anything he said. Connie loved him, and that love had always gotten her into trouble.

"Let's get out of here and get this pretty lady something to eat," Lawrence teased and offered an arm that Connie happily took.

—

As Connie walked out of the alley with Lawrence, Manny could not help but take notice. There were so many beautiful women all over the city, even more when the sun set, but Connie Murphy was fine. Rumor had it she had taken a job with Porter, and many were going to be there to see what was under those hideous dresses she always wore.

"Manny, are you listening?" Betty Tyler asked as she kneeled in front of him.

"I am not paying you to talk," he spat and took the back of her head, motioning her to continue.

Connie was not the only fine piece of ass in this part of the city. There was that lovely schoolteacher Sarah Monroe and that college student Cameron Mitchell, who always seemed to swoon over the O'Malley brothers. Yeah, there was enough of a selection around here to get anyone off, but as he finished with a stiff grunt, he pushed Betty away and adjusted himself.

"You don't need to be a dick!" Betty yelled as Manny threw a few coins at her.

"That is for talking," he said and walked away.

Manny left the raving prostitute screaming in the distance, but she had a habit, one that needed money. That meant whenever he needed a good suck, she would be the one to go to. Betty would do anything for money and had the scars to prove it.

"If you piss off the whore, she will cause a problem," Conner McDonald said as he leaned up against his car.

"Shove it, McDonald," Manny replied as Conner chuckled.

"Did I hit a nerve?"

"Want me to hit something to make you nervous?" Manny retorted and took larger steps towards Conner.

"I would love to see you try."

"Calm down, both of you," Porter commanded from inside the car.

Conner only grunted at the command and got into the back seat of the car, while Manny sat in the driver's seat. The three of them did not say a word as Manny started the car and pulled into the dust-filled streets. Even though the engine was loud, and the summer heat added to the uncomfortable conditions, this was home. Conner handed the older gentleman a list, one that was of the utmost importance.

"The shipment from across the pond is ready to move," Conner whispered to avoid Manny's listening ears.

"Local?" Porter asked.

"On schedule. The moonshine shit the hill boys produce is still popular enough that we can charge full price without worrying about a stocking shortage."

"Is this all?" Porter inquired with concern in his voice.

"It is what we usually bring in Boss."

Porter had no trouble flaunting the wealth he had gained over the years. The Prohibition was good for business. Too good, which made it more dangerous if he continued. At one time, Porter owned all the taverns in the city, and when they forced him to close, he consolidated and repurposed those buildings. They were empty according to the city, at least during the day, but at night, those black-out windows came alive. But this list was not what he was promised.

"I need more," Porter instructed and handed the list back to Conner.

"More?"

"Did I stutter?"

"Detective Colins is cracking down hard on the roads. Even the side roads are seeing more activity. I need a full week to reposition the shipments."

"You have until tonight."

"Don't forget you have your meeting with Paul Daniels this afternoon," Conner reminded him as Porter growled.

Paul Daniels was the secretary to the mayor of Boston. It was unusual but not unheard of to have a male secretary.

Paul's methods for getting things done were anything but legal, but he was very good at covering his tracks. A talent many took advantage of when they had no other solution to their problems.

In hearing Paul Daniels's name, Manny gripped the steering wheel hard. The situation of how he treated Manny's sister, Gretchen, was still a sore spot. Inappropriate touches should have put him behind bars, but he knew too many people that he was almost untouchable.

"Speak. I cannot read minds," Porter said.

"Daniels cannot be trusted," Conner whispered.

"That bit of knowledge I already know," Porter snapped as Manny cleared his throat.

"Sir, there has been talk of a Lawrence Murphy getting into the business and getting a crew together," Manny said. The news didn't surprise Porter, but he was upset he didn't hear about it until now.

"Is that all you got for me?" Porter asked.

"It is a small-time ring; it will flame out in a few weeks," Manny speculated.

"We've already alerted Detective Colins's new task force anonymously to their dealings. It will take the heat away from you,"

Conner said and glared at Manny for talking.

His crew had a system. Conner was the one in charge, to make all the decisions and always report to the boss. Manny was closer to him in a sense of loyalty and trust, but he asked Manny to be their driver, so that he wouldn't open his big mouth.

"Lawrence Murphy, you said his name was?" Porter asked.

"Yes, Boss," Conner replied.

Murphy. The name they give all those bastard children in that run-down state house a few blocks away. He had a Murphy in his employment, in fact, supposed to be starting tonight. There was no mistake this Lawrence Murphy thought he was so clever, but he would show little Connie what it meant to try and steal from him.

—

The car drove past many buildings on the main street. One of those buildings was City Hall, home to many political and law offices. Manny glanced at the southern belle, one he had the pleasure of watching from a distance, but when he saw Detective Colins talking to her, he kept his focus forward as he slowly drove past them.

"I will be fine on my own, Uncle; I have been in this city long enough to know my way around," Linda Bishop said as her colorful sundress moved in the morning wind.

"Linda, baby, regardless, Boston is a city filled with crime. I know you wanted to surprise me with this visit, but I am going to have someone bring you home." He was interrupted when a familiar face approached them.

"Good morning, Detective, Miss Bishop," the sickly-looking man said as Linda gave him a little curtsy in greeting.

"Mr. Daniels," Detective Colins said. Rather than dismiss the man, he had an idea.

"If I may, Mr. Daniels, I am late for a meeting. Would you mind making sure my niece gets home safely?" he asked as Paul smiled.

"Of course, I do not mind," he answered and offered an arm.

Linda did not like the man; no woman ever had a good first impression of him. His addiction to opioids not only rotted his teeth but also made him look older than he really was. Regardless, he was trusted, and when Detective Benjamin Colins walked away in a hurry, Paul turned to the lovely woman at his side as they both started to walk.

"Tell me, Miss Bishop, how are you this fine morning?" he asked. Linda was trying so hard not to scrunch up her nose at his foul-smelling breath.

"Wonderful, thank you for asking."

"It was nice of you to surprise your uncle, but he is right; this city can be dangerous."

"I can take care of myself," Linda said bluntly as they both fell silent.

Linda's eyes tried to find anything to distract her from her current situation. They looked to every window they passed and the buildings that held them. This city was vibrant and alive even if it seemed dark and full of despair. The buildings held the same neutral tones of red, brown, or gray. The faces outside these structures did not add to its appeal. Everyone was either in a hurry or had nowhere to go.

—

"Here you are," Sarah Monroe said as she handed a man huddled against the brick wall a small bag.

"Thank you kindly," he replied when he realized who it was.

A kind face. It was rare to see them around these parts, but a few people came down to the alleys and helped those in need. Cameron was supposed to be with Sarah today. Sarah had promised her father she would not go out on her weekly deliveries alone, but Cameron was busy, always busy.

Sarah was lucky. Her parents still had their jobs and never had an addiction to the one thing that was polluting this city. It was hard for her to walk by every day and do nothing. That sparked her to want to hand out food, water, or clothing she received as donations from others.

Each homeless person or family had a similar story. They got further behind on their rent due to job loss or harsh circumstances. Money was getting tighter, and with the restriction on alcohol, the need for the illegal substance made gatherings to spend money more common. No matter how much the government said it was helping, they never saw the reward for their hard work.

CHAPTER TWO

It was filthy. A place of cheap beer, stale cigarettes, and women. This was a place no one would come to work unless they were in desperate need or cash. A place that Connie had every right to want to run away from, but she promised Lawrence. A promise she was dreading, even now.

"So, you are the new hire," a ghastly older woman said as the cigarette smoke filled the small room.

Do not cough. Do not wrinkle your nose. Do not throw up. Those three statements were playing repeatedly in Connie's mind. She was terrified. This smell, she hated it but tried not to show it.

"Yes, ma'am," Connie replied, scared out of her ever-living mind.

It was not what she was expecting. The individual who met her at the corner of her building was old and smelled of stale cigarettes. He did not speak much but led her to this foreclosed bar, one that looked dead on the outside. When Connie slowly walked to the alley towards the back, she was immediately taken in by this woman who was now judging every imperfection her body had to offer.

"What?" Connie asked sheepishly.

"Your tits are too small," the woman blurted while Connie slowly crossed her arms to hide them.

"I'm—" Connie started to say but was interrupted.

"I was not done. Never interrupt me. Do you understand?"

"Yes, ma'am," Connie whispered.

"Good. As I was saying, your tits are too small. There is nothing we can do about that. A little more fat on your bones will give your goods some girth, but we have this to work with tonight." The haggard woman motioned to Connie. "Take the white dress on the door, and we will do something about that monstrosity of hair on top of your head."

That woman's voice shook Connie to her very core. She knew the outfit they would force her to wear would be ridiculously small and reveal everything. There was nothing she could do. Connie had made a promise to Lawrence, and if she did not keep that promise, he would be angry with her.

Connie took off her long plaid skirt and blouse. The room they forced her to change in was a closet, barely big enough to move with a curtain as a door. Looking down at herself, she wanted to cry. This wasn't what she wanted to do.

"Hurry up!" the woman yelled.

Her skin revealed the bruises and scars of trying to get her next meal. There was a time, desperate times where she would do anything and immediately regretted it. The only thing that made her any different from Betty Tyler was Betty boasted and bragged about what she did. That woman didn't care what anyone thought of her, a talent Connie did not possess.

"You can do this…" she whispered to herself.

She needed this job, and Lawrence was willing to risk her ability to pay rent on his stupid idea for a business. Connie was smarter than this, she knew she should run away, but what choice did she have? She did not want Lawrence upset with her. With that thought placed in her mind, Connie slipped on the dress.

"What is taking so long?" the haggard woman bellowed.

Connie suppressed a yelp of surprise and gave out a sigh. Slowly, she looked at the sheer white stocking in her hand and put them on over her long legs. With each piece she added, the frilly dress that would show everything if she bent over, the white heels and even the fake pearls, she became someone she did not recognize.

"You're going to make me late, and I am never late!" the woman yelled as Connie slowly emerged from behind the curtain.

The old woman made no comment on how she looked.

Immediately, Connie was dragged in front of a mirror and forced to sit down. It was as if she were a doll, being dressed up to the owner's approval. A doll, for the eyes of the men laughing on the other side of the wall.

"We can hide most of this hair behind a feather or two…" the woman mumbled as Connie watched her dark curls disappear.

"I am sorry," Connie muttered.

"Shut your mouth!" she snapped as ashes from her cigarette fell into Connie's hair.

"Yes, ma'am."

The band that was placed around her head matched the material of the dress. It was flexible yet tight. That band would not fall off even if she had to move suddenly, but the feather in front hid the shorter hairs that were uneven. It was a mess, and when the woman grabbed some scissors, Connie frowned.

It was only a few locks of hair. Connie watched them fall to the floor, and a tear escaped. They were completely changing her, erasing the woman she was to create this monster. Snip. Every time she heard the scissors and saw her hair fall, Connie wanted to cry.

They gave her no option but to submit. When she was done with the makeover, the woman pulled her towards the exit. The clicking of the heels was slowly drowned out by the laughter that was coming from the other room. Connie was absolutely terrified.

"I don't know what to do," Connie said as she stood in the doorway.

She gave Connie a tray and thrusted her deeper into the doorway facing the crowd. They gave her no training or advice. Nothing. All this woman did was dress her up and expect her to know everything about this job. When Connie didn't move, she felt the sharp sting of the cane on her thighs.

"Go!" the woman commanded.

She had no choice. With a deep breath and a smile, Connie took her first step into this world. It was madness. The amount of cigarette smoke clouded the air above as the sound of laughter, music, and glasses clinking together showed the party before her was slowly getting started.

Everyone who was here was those who could pay to enter. As long as they could keep a secret, everyone was able to enjoy the delights that the Eighteenth Amendment took away. A never-ending party, every night. All this new law did was make it more exciting to go out and have a good time. An excitement that was displayed on everyone's face.

"Don't stand there, move!" the older woman hollered, and Connie jumped at the sudden voice near her.

On her tray were cigarettes; she was to sell them to the customers. No big deal, right? Looking around, Connie tried to make herself feel more optimistic. At least she was not dancing on the stage or sitting in the lap of handsy men. It was a job; she could do this. The moment she took another step, she tripped and felt all eyes were on the new girl.

———

No one was paying her any attention, or at least Connie thought. Porter was watching carefully from across the room, analyzing the news of her relation to Lawrence Murphy, the man who wanted to put his name in this game. Porter refused to allow any competition to exist for long, he had to choose the perfect time to attack.

"She seems capable," Conner said as he and Porter looked to Connie.

"We will see," Porter replied and took a sip of his whisky.

"You could have her killed and be done with it."

"Hmm…I wanted to see how far she was willing to go." Porter took another sip of the drink in his hand.

The crowd was lively as he expected, and with every step, Miss Connie Murphy was either tripping over her feet or bumping into a customer. This was his establishment. Even though someone told him to close his front doors, it did not mean Porter could not open the back one.

It took all of two months to reorganize and make it so anyone with money, influence, or trade could fill their habit, no matter what it was. All he asked for was secrecy, and for no one to steal his business.

"She isn't bad looking either," Conner mentioned.

"She isn't a whore," Porter said.

The whores who ventured around, greeting every gentleman and the occasional lady, were under his employment. Porter was in the business of entertainment, and he did not judge based on your preference. But Connie, she was in the most revealing thing he had that did not mark her as someone you could touch. He was very firm that his employees were not to be touched unless they said otherwise.

"The distillery that is providing Lawrence is new, mostly in moonshine or hogwash of brandy. By letting his ego grow, that boy will make a mistake and get the wrong person's attention," Conner informed.

"Good," was Porter's only reply.

"Is it too bold? Or stupid for Lawrence to put a fellow orphan in the lion's den?" Conner asked, amused by Connie's tumbles.

"Yes," Porter said, distracted by his own thoughts.

"Are you going to have her taken care of?" Conner asked.

Conner McDonald was in the business of money. He did not care who he had to hurt to get the job done. Death did not bother him, but watching Connie, he could not help but feel pity for the poor girl. She should be pushing a library cart or teaching at a schoolhouse; this establishment would break her before she ever saw a profit.

"I need you to intercept Lawrence Murphy's shipment and destroy it all," Porter finally said, finishing the drink in his hand.

"You're sending a very strong message."

"If you allow them to start small, they will eventually know enough people and that may create a challenge." Porter turned the moment Detective Benjamin Colins walked up to the bar.

The man looked tired, and his tie was loosened to show he was done for the day. Without asking, he took the empty glass out of Porter's hand and put it on the bar table behind them. It took the bartender only a moment to refill that glass, and when he did, the detective downed its entire contents.

—

This whole viewpoint of alcohol was going to destroy any ambition the detective had for doing this job. The politicians were out of control, yet it was the small-time speakeasy owners like Porter that were in the crossfire. It was the idea of freedom that held promise, but the execution was severely flawed.

"Take a walk, McDonald," Porter said, and Conner did not think twice about the command.

Once the glass was put on the table, it was refilled. This time, however, the detective took a seat before nursing the glass that Porter once held. It was a long day for both men, and Porter waited patiently to hear what was troubling the man beside him.

"I hate that kid!" Colins finally exclaimed.

"You're mad he is sweet on your niece," Porter replied playfully.

"Piss off." The detective took another sip of his drink.

"A lot of people have their eyes on her, but Conner is a good kid," Porter said before glancing over at his friend and frowning.

The detective's jacket was covered in mud, and his hands showed a fight. It was never easy for those who were trying to do good. But people would do what they needed to survive, even if it meant an honest man was the one to get hurt.

"I don't want your pity, Port. Shove it up your ass," Colins finally said and took a sip of the drink in his hand.

"Why do you continue to be in a place that is destroying you? You and I can rule this city; all you need to do is say the word." The

detective could not help but laugh.

"After my wife died, you were the only one that was there for me. Through the funeral and all the bills from her illness. If I did not have you, I do not know what I would have done." Colins took another sip.

"But now, I have Linda, and she is too innocent to be stained by this place," Colins added and let out a sigh of defeat.

Porter gently put a hand on his friend's shoulder as his eyes glanced to Connie. That girl was not fit for this job, but she needed the money and Porter never turned away someone in need. He watched as she bumped into yet another customer.

—

"Oh my goodness, I am so sorry," Connie exclaimed as her entire tray fell right onto Finnick's lap.

Finnick and Patrick were exhausted. Between the store and the alcohol run they did only a few hours ago, they were ready to sleep. The need for money was the reason the boys lived a double life.

Their father was not doing well; between the debt for the store and his medical bills, money was always a problem but when

Finnick looked at Connie, it seemed he was not the only one having a bad day.

"No worries," he said and picked up a few cartons to put back on her tray.

"I am such a mess. These heels are making it so I cannot walk straight." Connie whined as she continued. "Everyone has been awful, and I haven't made a single sale."

Finnick looked to his brother for some guidance. The man knew nothing about how to calm a woman down, but rather than taking enjoyment in his brother's situation, Patrick's focus was across the room.

 His eyes fell on Detective Benjamin Colins, a man everyone knew very well.

"I don't smoke, sorry, lass," Finnick finally replied.

Patrick knew all law enforcement officers were crooked one way or another. Everyone had to sneak around, and it was no secret that Detective Colins was under Porter's protection. They were friendly, and no one could walk in here and demand an audience with the boss like Colins could. Porter had no friends; they were a liability, but it seemed like there was an exception to every rule.

"Do you smoke?" Connie asked as Patrick was pulled out of his thoughts.

"No, lass, but I do have a question for you…" Patrick paused, pretending he didn't already know her name.

"Connie," she answered.

"Connie, why is Lawrence Murphy's housemate working in Porter's joint?" Patrick asked, not dancing around the one question everyone had.

"I. Uh..."

"Word on the street is he is putting his hat in the business and will be Conner's competition, and everyone knows he works for Porter."

The woman had wide eyes and looked like a little rabbit about to run. When she turned, she bumped into someone. The O'Malley brothers could not help but laugh. Patrick knew how to get her to go away, but it was sad to see her in such a place.

"You're mean," Finnick said to his brother as Patrick raised his glass, knowing full well they needed to be home soon.

—

It did not matter how loud anyone was; that laughter and music Was heard all down the street. Every police officer who was patrolling heard the noise but never investigated. It was all because of a deal Porter made to be sure all his bases were covered, but Betty Tyler was not amused this evening.

"I said I want—" a man argued as Betty held up her long finger.

"Go away," she demanded.

That man was not pleased, and when he took a step towards her, Betty held up the knife she always carried. She was a woman of the streets. It was not the most glamorous profession, but it put food in her belly and a roof over her head. The reason she could work so close to Porter's business was because Betty was good at getting information, and with her late morning customer, Betty knew if she lingered long enough, Porter would come out and pay for what she knew.

"You have something for me, Betty?" Porter asked as he appeared before her.

He always smelled so clean. She wanted to be clean but knew nobody really cared how she smelled or what she looked like. The information she could get when they were knee-deep was something Porter appreciated. An appreciation that got her the protection she needed to stay alive.

"Paul Daniels," she spat, and Porter rolled his eyes.

Paul Daniels was everyone's headache. An unnecessary individual at City Hall causing problems everywhere he went. He was known to use unorthodox methods to get legislation passed. Regardless if he was a simple secretary, Paul Daniels thought he controlled everything.

He was good enough at covering his tracks and making sure people did not talk. By Betty saying his name, it meant it came directly

from Paul Daniels's mouth, and any information that could be used against the man was worth the price.

"Speak," Porter ordered.

"He plans on hitting the O'Malley brother's place, the grocery store," she said, and that got Porter's attention.

"There should be no reason he would target the establishment." Porter held up a rolled wad of bills to keep her talking.

"The cleanup. The community is not following the guidelines set by City Hall, who wants to clean up the streets. The community feeds the homeless, and the individuals who take expired or outdated goods and hand them out will attract more homeless. With the O'Malley brothers' father becoming sick, the community is rallying together to make sure the store stays afloat. That type of support towards a non-government official is seen as a rally."

"Get to the point."

"They worry about riots. Not that the Eighteenth Amendment has created an uprising, but people who gain the public's affection become noticed. They need to comply, or Paul Daniels will do what he always does to close their doors forever," Betty explained as Porter tossed her the bills.

"Next time you are with Paul Daniels, inform me. I want to speak to this man unofficially; our real talks are long overdue." He walked back into the bar.

"You're welcome!" Betty called while bending down to pick up her money.

Porter paid her well, which made it so she would never lie to him. Everyone knew what would happen if Porter learned you lied to him. The body was never found, and the family is forced to relocate or suffer the same fate.

—

"What did your little informant say?" Detective Colins asked, clearly intoxicated when Porter returned.

"Finish your drink," Porter responded, not wanting to talk about it in the open.

Porter looked at the O'Malley brothers and thought about the proper way to approach this. Everyone knew their father was gentle and would help anyone. That was extremely hard to find in this world, and his boys were honorable and loyal to him. If something happened to their father or his store, Porter would lose his two best runners, and morale of that block would shatter. Porter needed to deal with Daniels without the brothers knowing about it, which would be hard, but he would think of something.

CHAPTER THREE

"You are not looking too good, Detective. Any late-night habits you wish to share?" Paul Daniels spat with a smug expression.

City Hall never slept, nor did the people who worked within it find peace. Everyone had been in meetings all week. Senator Murphy was adamant about making the war on crime his campaign towards a future presidential bid, and it was making all law enforcement work nonstop. It did not help that other officials, mainly ones with Paul Daniels in their employ, were also on board with this campaign. With a very mixed group of citizens in this city, the topics had no easy solution.

"Did you hear me?" Daniels asked, speaking louder.

"What do you want Daniels?" Detective Colins grumbled, obviously hung over from last night's talks with Porter.

"I said, you're not looking too good," Daniels said, repeating himself but not giving Colins any chance of comeback before he spoke again. "You, an American born such as yourself, seem to favor the Irish. I am surprised."

"Do you have a point?" Colins asked.

"They are vermin that came here and took over. You are the only police officer I have met that doesn't seem to have a problem with them," Daniels whispered, taking a step towards Colins.

"They are people, too," Colins said, taking a sip of the water that appeared in his hand moments ago.

"Correct, but they are not our people. These individuals were not born here; they don't deserve the same rights we have," Daniels added, taking yet another step towards Colins.

Americans feared immigration. They were worried about the job market as well as the housing being sought after by those who were not born in this country. It did not matter what the facts stated or how there was enough to go around; they feared the unknown, and that was what the whole premise of these meetings was all about.

"Take a look around you, Daniels. We are right in the heart of Irish Immigration and all I see are hard-working people trying to provide for their families," Colins emphasized, but Daniels only gave him one of those grins that was followed by trouble.

"All I see are illegals trying to take what is ours. They have their own country with their own problems. We do not need it following us here."

Detective Colins was usually calm and could take the criticism of others, but something in him snapped. It was the very moment a group of children entered the hall that caused him to grab Daniels's collar forcefully.

As Colins pinned the man against the wall, people continued to walk by them as if nothing was happening. Even when the detective got into Daniels's personal space, he did not let him go and made sure to look as intimidating as possible.

"Listen to me very carefully, Daniels," Colins started.

"I am listening," Daniels replied.

"Leave these people alone," Colins hissed between his teeth.

"Or what?" Daniels countered, that smirk still not leaving his face.

"They are not the ones who are causing the disrupt and mayhem. They are not the ones making alcohol illegal and shipping it around the country. They are not the corrupt politicians who think they know what is best." Detective Colins gripped onto the man's clothing tighter.

"But they are a driving force in what makes it so successful—"

Colins pulled him forward, only to push him back hard against the wall once more.

"If I hear you caused trouble, I will take immense pleasure in putting you in a cell," Colins said, but the conversation was interrupted when Senator Murphy walked up to the two of them with a displeased look spread across his face.

"Trouble, gentlemen?"

Both men looked at the senator and frowned. If there was a more corrupted politician with a one-track mind, it was Senator

Hamilton Murphy. He was sympathetic when he needed to be, but his look showed he was curious enough to call in the authorities if needed. He cared only about himself and had no interest in resolving the current dispute.

"No trouble, right, Detective?" Daniel stated.

"No, no trouble." Detective Colins finally let go of Daniels who slowly straightened his shirt.

"Good. Detective Colins, a word please," the senator ordered as Daniel walked away gracefully, leaving the two men to talk business.

Colins watched as Daniels walked away as if their encounter had never happened. Porter knew of the troubles that man could cause

and Colins was there to pick up the pieces. No one liked him, yet he had the entire world eating out of his hand.

"What can I do for you, Senator?" Colins asked, keeping it professional as possible.

"Cut the shit, Ben. You and I both know if things continue to go the way they are, we will have a riot on our hands." He spoke low enough so that no one around him would hear his words.

"We are going to keep this professional, Senator Murphy," Colins insisted in a calm voice.

The senator looked around him slowly. Daniels was everywhere, and even though he was nowhere to be seen, that did not mean he would not overhear what was about to be said. A long few minutes of uncomfortable silence passed before the senator thought it was safe to speak.

"You and I are well past professional," Senator Murphy said as Colins shrugged.

"I have no idea what you are referring to."

"It is those O'Malley boys and all their kind that are causing this mess. If you had done your job and arrested them like ordered, we would not be here today."

"There is no evidence linking the O'Malley brothers to any illegal activity."

"Evidence?" the senator snapped as a group of children ran by them.

"It is all speculation. A witch hunt, and let me remind you how badly that turned out a few hundred years ago,"
Detective Colins said as both men fell quiet when more children walked past them.

"I—"

"Miss Monroe, who are these men?" a schoolchild asked as he pointed to the senator and detective.

It was obvious by the two men's outfits what positions they held. The large over-coat covered Detective Colins's pistol, but he has been seen around the neighborhood enough that one would know his position. The senator's polished suit and straight tie was a signal of a political profession, but when a woman walked in front of the students, she smiled at the men before her.

Sarah Monroe was a gentle soul. She had been the elementary school teacher for all the school-aged children for the past ten years. Between that and her volunteer work, everyone loved her. She was always calm and understanding, tall and plain. Nothing about her stood out and made it so she could hide well within her group of children.

"He has nice shoes," a little girl observed and pointed to the senator.

"That one has a long coat like a police officer," another child said.

"I think the taller one is handsome," a girl spoke as all the boys around her pretended to be disgusted by her observation.

"Children, you are looking at our very own Senator Hamilton Murphy and Detective Benjamin Colins. These two individuals are responsible for keeping us safe."

"What is a senator?" a child blurted.

"Is it something to do with toilets?"

"Or maybe he is in a magazine!"

As the questions regarding Senator Murphy continued, they also looked at Detective Colins. They were innocent children, and both men knew they could not yell at them to be quiet. When they looked to Ms. Monroe for assistance, she gave them a small smile and shrugged.

"Do you carry a gun?" one asked.

"Have you shot anyone?"

"Did you kill them?"

A calmness overflowed the detective as he held up his hands in surrender. He could never say no to these delightful children. Their clothing was too big and in bad need of repair. Miss Monroe worked within the low-income communities, but she never judged anyone based on their income or ability to care for their families.

"Now, children, Detective Colins works very hard to keep the streets safe for everyone," Senator Murphy began, but Colins bent down to meet the children eye to eye, making sure they were paying attention.

"I do carry a gun, and I use it to protect myself as well as those who need it. What do we do if a stranger approaches us?"

"What if there is a shootout?" a little boy asked.

"The pistol you carry will never stand a chance against a Tommy gun," another said as the other pretended to shoot.

They were an obvious distraction from the busy schedule many people had. It was time for them to move along, and before more questions left their mouths, their teacher slowly shooed them along. With a simple whistle and a slight nudge, they continued their walk, observing and speaking whatever was on their minds.

"If you are not firm with the children when they are boys, they will grow into uncontrollable men," Senator Murphy spat as he walked away.

The world did not stop. Colins watched the senator depart, and even though it would take longer to get back to his office, he walked in the opposite direction to avoid any more confrontation. He would not let one man ruin his day.

—

"Idiot," Senator Murphy mumbled as he sped away from Colins.

Everything and everyone were causing him problems. Murphy needed to focus, needed to clean up the crime in Boston because if he did, it was a sure victory. The presidency would be his, but as he walked into his office, he was surprised to see Lawrence, the one person he did not want to be associated with anymore.

"What the hell are you doing?" the senator yelled but bit his lip to avoid any more outbursts that would draw attention.

Lawrence looked like he had been in a fight. Blood stained his face, and his clothing was ripped. The sorry excuse for a jacket that was obviously too big made him stand out. He could not hide the evidence of the fight even if he tried.

"I am in trouble, Ham," Lawrence explained on the verge of tears, but Hamilton refused to listen.

"I do not have time for this."

"I really need your help."

"I do not care!"

They were not children anymore. Hamilton grew up with Lawrence and Connie. He was familiar with circumstances of being poor and hungry. This man fought for the education he deserved and a place in the world that wanted to throw him away. He was so close to getting everything he dreamed of and now that Lawrence was here, he could ruin everything.

"I thought I could start up—" Lawrence tried to say, but the senator stalked around the room and grabbed Lawrence's jacket.

"Shut up!" the senator yelled.

"It was going to be easy. I would start in the mountains and—"

"Shut your goddamn mouth! You will ruin everything for me. I want no association with you, nothing. Do not come around here again, you nor Connie. Both of you are dead to me!"

Lawrence remembered when they were boys. When Hamilton was nothing more than a scrawny kid who always got beaten up for being outspoken. Now, Hamilton was big and filled out his overpriced suit. Never would Lawrence forget where he came from, and he refused to let him throw them away.

"Porter attacked my run," Lawrence said.

"I said I do not want to hear it!" the senator snapped, gripping onto Lawrence's jacket tighter.

"He killed some of my crew, and now, no one wants to work with me. I owe too many people money, and if I do not pay, they will come after all of us," Lawrence retorted, and as Senator Murphy heard that, he punched Lawrence hard in the face.

Crunch. There was no question that the impact broke something. Lawrence fell from the senator's grasp and hit the floor. Blood slowly seeped from his nose, but the look of betrayal was real on his face.

"We are a family, Hamilton. You, Connie, and I. We may not be blood, but we are family by circumstance. You cannot shut us out because you're embarrassed!"

"No one will believe I associate with scum such as you," he yelled, and it was loud enough to bring a knock at his door.

"I am not going anywhere, Hamilton," Lawrence reminded his brother and slowly stood, walking towards the open window of the office.

Thankfully for Lawrence, the open window was at ground level. Hamilton was disappointed the drop would not hurt, but he pushed

Lawrence out the window and made sure that low life fell the moment

the door opened. No one could see him.

"Are you all right, sir?" Gretchen asked as she walked into the room.

Senator Murphy closed the window and latched it. He would make a note of how easy it was for Lawrence to break in. That meant security to this whole building was lax. Someone would pay for what happened in this room today; he would make sure of it.

"Yes." Senator Murphy took a moment to straighten himself before turning to face Gretchen.

"This is a reminder, Senator, that you have a meeting in thirty minutes."

"Thank you, Gretchen." With that, Gretchen nodded and left the room as quickly as she had entered it.

This was bad. If Lawrence got into trouble, it would not take any reporter long to find that he had a connection to him. They were boys, their circumstances were out of his control, but if he had connection to any crime, the title of Mr. President would become out of his reach. He had to fix this but did not know where to begin.

CHAPTER FOUR

Lawrence was in trouble. Shit. No matter how many times he replayed what happened the night before, there was no way out of this. It was an ambush, one he never saw coming.

The contact he made in the hills needed to travel a full day to get to the drop point. Lawrence had no real transporters, not like Conner and the O'Malley brothers. That made it so Lawrence had to go by himself. It was supposed to be easy, yet; it went so wrong.

"Where the fuck did it go all wrong?" Lawrence yelled.

"Move along now!" a patrolman hollered, which caused Lawrence to move deeper into the alley.

He had borrowed a car from a friend. It had gotten to the point where the need for wheels was a must but the money to get one was still short. He had exhausted all his options with cash that he was left with borrowing vehicles. Thousands of dollars were owed for supplies, and the rest of the money went to the hill town boys because they demanded the payment upfront. He should have known the signs of an ambush, but he had mistakenly gotten cocky about his ability to do this all by himself.

The men from the hills had come on their trucks, like they did the previous week. It was not full like he paid for, which was suspicious. Lawrence made sure to order the max in case he could not afford to next week.

To top off his problems, the truck that had come was painted over, and all signs of their farm were covered. That was another bad sign. He was alone, Lawrence knew he should not have come alone, and when he saw the Tommy guns, he hid underneath his car knowing what was about to happen.

Pop. Pop. Pop.

It had been an ambush, an attack. Lawrence recognized the driver instantly; it was someone under Porter's employment. This was a message to not get involved in his business. As the shells fell to the dirt road, another vehicle pulled up. That was when Lawrence knew his problems were not over.

"What seems to be the problem here, boys?" a local deputy had said that day as he approached the scene.

It had still been dark out that night, both gentlemen hanging from the truck and the driver did not move. They did not attempt to hide the evidence that they were the ones that fired. The crunching of the deputy's boots caused Lawrence to frown.

The deputy had not drawn his weapon or made any indication that he was going to act regarding the gunmen or the truck. All the deputy did was walk closer and closer to Lawrence. When he crouched down, it was clear which side he was on, and Lawrence looked to the deputy, terrified.

"This road doesn't belong to you," was all the deputy had said, and that phrase played over and over in Lawrence's head as he remembered the beating.

He had been immediately greeted by a fist along with laughter.

It was coming from both the truck and the deputy as he was pulled out from under and kicked hard in the stomach. Lawrence knew if he fought back, he would have been arrested.

He remembered every strike. How each kick, each punch felt against him. Even though he tried to protect his head, they still gave him black eyes and a busted lip. No mercy was shown. It was only till they grew tired that the beatings stopped.

As he lain there for what felt like hours, he heard them talking. The sun was starting to rise, and he knew that if he moved, they would kill him. But the information he learned was enough to know that Porter was behind all of this.

"We tracked the last shipment and know which boys supplied his goods," the deputy had explained.

"What are you going to do about it?" the driver asked.

"I will personally pay them a visit, so you can tell your boss my debt is paid."

"The boss will let you know when the debt is paid," was the driver's response, and the tone was not very friendly.

Lawrence had coughed more than he ever had before and rolled onto his side. The dust from the departing vehicles got into his face and caused him to sneeze. The car he borrowed was totaled. He did not need to look at the car to know that he owed yet someone else money, the one thing he didn't have.

The one person he had left that could help had thrown him out. The bruises from the beating were still raw, and the blood was dried on his clothes and skin. As he relived that night repeatedly, he made it into his apartment.

"Larry, open the door!" someone barked from the other side, and he knew immediately who that voice belonged to.

It was the owner of the car. He was the only man who ever called him Larry. Because Lawrence did not return the vehicle this morning, the owner came looking for it. The fire escape was the only way he could get in and out of his apartment. Lawrence was two months behind on rent and had too many people looking for him.

"Shit," he muttered and headed towards the fire escape but was met with a very upset Connie.

"It was awful!" she whined loud enough that the person on the other side of the door yelled louder.

"I do not have time for this, Connie. I went to see Hamilton, and he threw me out," Lawrence said as the knocks on his door turned into punches trying to break it down.

"Oh my goodness! How much trouble are you in?"

"Come on." He jumped through the window, leading her down the fire escape.

They both needed to go someplace Porter's henchmen would not hear them. It also did not help that the people Lawrence owed money to would be out looking for him. It was a risk, but when he pulled Connie to the back alley of O'Malley Grocery, she had a worried expression on her face.

"How bad is it?" she asked gently and reached forward to touch the large bruise on his face.

"What can you tell me about Porter?" he asked, wanting to talk business over the problem that was his life.

"The clothing they had me in was horrendous, but now I can finally walk in those shoes. Everyone is there, Lawrence; politicians, cops, even other gang members, and no one dares to do a damn

thing to each other under Porter's roof."

"How does he run it?"

"He runs a tight show, and I have no idea how you will compete with that." Lawrence frowned at her statement.

"That does not help me, Connie."

"I do not know what you need from me, Lawrence. There was so much going on I do not know where to begin."

"When are his runs?"

"I do not know."

"Who was there so I can blackmail them? I need specific names!" he shouted as movement behind the neighboring store caused them both to turn.

Vincent Sullivan was a worker at the clothing store next door. He always looked proper for the job, and his hands were uncalloused. The tall, thin man would never make it in a world filled with criminals and violence. He was too good for that but rather than look at the two of them, he threw away the trash and walked back into the store as if nothing was happening.

"If I give you names, they can trace it back to me. They will kill me," Connie said as Lawrence looked down at her.

"Please, Connie," he said as she looked away, ashamed.

"Detective Benjamin Colins was there." Lawrence held the bridge of his nose to try to remain calm.

"We all know they are friendly. I need something more or at least proof I can hold over Colins's head to get his protection," he seethed as Connie looked at him with a blank stare.

Connie thought about what he was asking. There were so many people going in and out of that place.

Between the music, dancing, and all the interactions, it was hard to keep track of everyone. When she thought of something, she grabbed Lawrence's arm and beamed promise.

"Manny Laird was there. He was intoxicated and yelling at the top of his lungs about how Gretchen, a worker at City Hall was in love with Finnick O'Malley. He hates the O'Malley's because his sister has showered them with gifts and letters with no response. He is acquainted with Paul Daniels, who also works at City Hall." she explained as Lawrence finally formed a smile.

It was perfect. The O'Malleys were the backbone to the transportation, and if they were taken out, the shipments would be affected. How to take them out was the real question. When he looked at Connie, she wanted to be told she did a good job. She needed the validation from him because all she ever wanted was to please him and he would use that to his advantage.

"You did good, Connie," he said as she jumped into his arms.

"Really?" she asked as Lawrence slowly pried her off him.

"Really."

"Oh, Lawrence, that makes me so glad."

"Listen to me very closely, Connie. I need you to talk to Betty Taylor for me," Lawrence said, and the reaction to the prostitute's name was a common one.

"Why would I talk to her?" Connie mumbled with a scrunched-up expression.

"She has served everyone and knows who to talk to in order to get this information to Paul Daniels." Lawrence held onto her shoulders to make sure she was paying attention.

"Why does it matter?" Connie asked, trying to find her way back to the happiness she felt only a few moments ago.

"Connie..." He let out a sigh.

"What do you want me to say?"

"Have her tell Manny that the O'Malleys are laughing at Gretchen. That her attempts to woo them were in vain and they enjoy the show. That way, he will overreact and go straight to Daniels. That man will do something about it and hopefully go over the top." Excitement spread across his face.

"Why do you want to hurt them? They have always been so nice."

"Don't you understand, Connie? They are the transportation, the muscle for Porter's day-to-day operation. If I can take them out, Porter's business would suffer."

Lawrence still had his hands on her shoulders. He squeezed them, a little too hard to get her to pay attention. Connie still had sympathy in her expression, so Lawrence squeezed a little harder. He needed her to understand.

"They are our enemy, Connie. Anyone who isn't us is our enemy. You need to understand that, or I will have no more use for you." He dug his fingers into her skin.

"You're hurting me…" she whimpered as he did not loosen his hold.

"Good. Maybe you will smarten up."

Lawrence had changed. As children, they were thick as thieves, and he looked out for everyone. But the older he got, the more trouble he got into. Between the drinking and gambling, Lawrence kept getting further and further into debt, and all his plans to make it big turned disastrous.

The two of them were going to buy a house and stay together, that was the plan. But when Hamilton went off to college, Lawrence grew cold. He learned the thrill of the cards, the taste of booze, and how poorly he could get away with treating women. His actions were going to kill him one day, but all Connie could do was nod and give him a hug, hoping this would not be the last time she would see him alive.

CHAPTER FIVE

"Right there, yes, like that." Manny groaned as he was once again in that dark alley, enjoying himself.

It had been a few days since Lawrence was dealt with, but that did not mean everyone was lax. Between his assignments from Conner and Porter, there was extraordinarily little time for Manny to find pleasure. As a result, he had to resort to a quick fuck in the alley.

It was hard to get a woman, one that utterly understood a man. They wanted attention, needed to be showered with gifts, and no man had the time for that. Betty was cheap and knew how to do her job very well. He was a regular, and the moment he pushed forward hard, he grunted. When Manny was finished, he pushed her away.

Betty had to clean up before she could do her assignment. When her mouth was not full and her face was semi-presentable, she looked up to Manny in disgust. There was no joy in what she did, and it made her job harder when the men were rude.

"Before you storm off, I have something you might be interested in learning," she swooned as Manny adjusted his pants.

"Not interested," he spat and reached into his pocket.

"Even if it is about the O'Malley brothers?" she said, and Manny froze in place.

He hated them. No number of lectures he had given Gretchen made her see how bad they were. Especially Finnick, that man looked right through her after she gave them so much. Food, small knick-knacks, letters, and other items that she could barely afford. There was one time when she stayed up late and made sure Finnick had a fresh glass of milk when they returned from their deliveries. It was disgusting, and any chance to give them a good smack was welcome.

"Tell me," Manny demanded.

"They laugh at her you know," Betty said.

"Who?"

"Gretchen. They throw away every letter she leaves unsigned. They know full well who they are from. How does it feel to have a sister who is the laughingstock of Porter's runners?"

Manny raised a fist.

"You touch me, my lips will be sealed, and you will never know the rest," Betty said, knowing how to handle a disgruntled customer.

"Speak." Manny slowly lowered his arm.

"They guess what she looks like underneath her skirt and determined she isn't worth the courting to get a piece of ass," Betty said with a smug grin on her face.

Connie wanted Manny mad. She paid Betty good money to make sure Manny left so pissed off that he would go straight to Daniels, demanding something be done. The expression on Manny's face showed she did her job, and the bills he threw at her showed the information was worth something.

"Nice doing business with you," Betty called out and watched him leave the alley ready to explode.

—

Gretchen had no idea what was about to happen. She was enjoying a lunch out with a close friend. Betty made sure not to bring her customers to a place where they would be caught, so the idea of her brother being upset currently did not cross her mind.

"Come on, Cameron, I barely get to see you anymore now that you are studying. Spill it! I need the gossip!" Gretchen whined as she looked across the table at Cameron, a friend she had forever.

"It is not that bad," Cameron replied.

These two were always close, had been since grade school, but when Gretchen got the job at City Hall, she decided not to further her education like Cameron. They were also very different in appearance. Gretchen felt she was nothing special with her dirty blonde hair and blue eyes, average height, and a little too much weight in all the wrong places.

Not like Cameron, tall with her mother's beautiful crème-color skin and exotic features. Those eyes were so dark, like her beautiful curly hair, and Gretchen wanted to be her. It was no wonder the boys always loved her.

"What do you want me to say, Gretchen? I am studying; there is no time for dating. I barely have enough time to meet up with you, but I made sure to make it happen," she said and winked.

Gretchen grumbled and took a sip of her ginger ale. Never once was Cameron too outspoken or caused a scene. Everyone loved her, and it was starting to annoy Gretchen on how perfect she was.

"There has to be at least someone you find attractive," Gretchen inquired and saw Cameron's eyes light up.

"Well…" she started.

"I knew it! Tell me!" Gretchen demanded.

"As you know, the Irishmen can be charmers when they want to be, and I guess one finally broke through the barrier."

"Who?" Gretchen asked.

"Well, you probably don't know them…." Cameron began and the screech that came out of Gretchen's mouth alerted the whole café.

"Them? There is more than one?" she screamed, and Cameron reached across the table to cover her mouth.

"Easy, let me explain before you jump to conclusions." Both women settled back down. "As you know, I moved back to the area once I got accepted into school. My roommate had her groceries delivered. At first, it was one man who was tall and had a full head of orange hair. He had a wonderful personality. His Irish accent was muddled; he said he moved to America when he was a boy."

As Cameron continued to explain, the facial expression on Gretchen was unreadable. She was talking about an O'Malley. There was no mistake about that. Only one place in the area delivers, and even though the Irish are dense in population, the grocery store was family-owned and run. Was it her Finnick?

The brothers were not twins, they were four years apart, but they looked so much alike. Cameron did not give enough detail on which one delivered to her apartment, but Gretchen prayed so hard it wasn't her Finny.

"What is his name?" Gretchen inquired.

Cameron was oblivious like always. She hummed to herself, sipping her ginger ale and swinging her legs back and forth in the chair. Everyone loved her, so she never had to learn to read people's expressions. An innocence that needed to be broken.

"I never asked, but a few weeks ago, my roommate and I went to the store where he works, and I saw his brother. I swear to you,

Gretchen, they must be twins because beauty can only be pure once and there were both super nice."

"Once, one of them walked me back to my apartment," she continued. "A different time, another one carried my bags to the trolly. He even bought me some candy. They are both super sweet."

Gretchen's heart broke instantly.

"Both of them?"

"Yup!"

They both liked her. It was obvious by the way she talked. Something happened in Gretchen that caused her to immediately stand and walk out. With no explanation, she ran as fast as she could towards City Hall. Her lunch break was almost over, and she needed to forget all she had heard.

Finnick, her Finny, loved another. Why couldn't it be her? She was so distressed by the news that she ran right into her brother and they both fell into a pile of trash alongside the street.

"Gretchen? What happened?" Manny asked.

"Why can't Finny love me, Manny?" Gretchen sobbed.

"Gretchen, I need you to tell me exactly what happened."

"I know I am not the prettiest, but I am not ugly. It is not fair; Cameron gets everything. Why can't it be me?" Manny held onto his sister, more determined than ever to see the O'Malleys hurt, or possibly dead for making his sister cry.

CHAPTER SIX

It took Gretchen a lot longer than he anticipated to pull herself together. She told him about lunch and how Cameron was in love with both O'Malley brothers. Sometimes, Manny's sister was dramatic and over the top, but seeing her so upset made his heart ache.

"What do you want?" Paul Daniels snapped as they met behind City Hall a few hours later.

"I want the O'Malley brothers gone. I am serious this time. No more bullshit," Manny said.

"Manny…"

"They are fucking around and leaving my sister in ruin."

"We have been over this. The O'Malley boys work for Conner, who works for Porter. If I hit them, it will ripple to the top and can make my life overly complicated."

"The store!" Manny blurted.

"Excuse me?"

"If you cannot go after the brothers, then hit their livelihood. Their pop thinks they are God's gift to the world and parades around about having a clean shop. Destroy the store!"

Daniels listened to his words and was now deep in thought. As the mayor's secretary, he attended every meeting, and the topic of the Eighteenth Amendment was a thorn in everyone's side. They had not found a solution to the Porter problem, and maybe this could work in everyone's favor.

"You both work for the same person. Their loss could affect your gain," Daniels explained.

"I do not care what happens to me. My sister needs to be avenged."

Porter's entire crew was tight and protected. It was that damned Detective Colins that had made Porter untouchable. But Manny did have a point. If the O'Malley brothers broke off on their own, they would not have Porter's protection, and it would be tremendous blow to his business.

"Give me time, and I will think of something," Daniels responded and turned, walking away.

Manny knew that answer was the best he would get. Daniels was twisted like that. He needed full deniability in any part of any crime to avoid capture. But he was as dirty as all the rest.

—

That night, everything was still. Individuals were in their homes, resting and enjoying time with their families. Even the O'Malley brothers relaxed in the apartment above the shop, but the sound of braking glass caught Finnick's attention.

"Did you hear that?" Finnick asked Patrick, who was sitting near him.

"Hear what?" Glass shattered again, and they both stood.

They were on the move. By the time both men were downstairs, a small fire had started in the middle of the store. It couldn't be caused by a lit candle or the stove in the corner; there was no mistake that the four masked individuals standing outside caused the flames before them.

"Go!" Patrick yelled as Finnick dashed out the door.

The entire store was made of wood, and a fire could destroy everything. Patrick grabbed the mop bucket in the corner and threw it on the fire. It did not stop; whatever accelerant they had used caused it to slowly grow and eat up the two displays in the middle of the store.

"Fuck!" Patrick yelled and looked around.

Finnick was already engaged in a fight with the four masked individuals. The grunts and punches pierced the calm night while Patrick pulled the curtains away from the windows. If he couldn't drown the fire out, he would smother it.

"Boys?" their father yelled from upstairs.

Their father didn't call down twice. By that time, the smoke had alerted him, and he was downstairs as fast as his frail body would let him.

"You bastard!" Finnick yelled and punched the second man who tried to add to the already growing fire.

"Don't let them throw any more in!" Patrick yelled to his brother through the window.

"No shit!" Finnick replied.

Broken glass from the window littered the streets, and the screams alerted the neighbors. Someone must have alerted the authorities by now, or at least they hoped. It would take a while for the vehicles to get here, and if there was another fire in the area, the store could be ash by the time they joined the party. But the one thing this community

loved more than a good party was a good fight.

"I called in for some reinforcements," Vincent yelled as he appeared by Finnick's side.

"Vinny?" Finnick asked, surprised to hear the man's voice.

Usually, the scrawny man would never start a fight or be in one, but this was personal. The entire block relied on each other for

business and attracting customers. If they lost the store, it would be devastating to every owner on the block.

"Stay back!" Finnick yelled as he received a punch to the face, that wasn't strong enough to knock him down.

"Stay down, you ugly bastard!" one of the masked men yelled.

"You should not have done that," Finnick threatened.

He grabbed the man's head and brought it directly against his own. When it made contact, Finnick showed no sign of pain on his face. His opponent, on the other hand, fell to the ground, unconscious, the moment he let the body go.

"I want to help!" Vincent called out as he received a punch to the face, too.

Unlike Finnick, Vincent was small and had never been in a fight. When the man hit the ground, Finnick growled. No one hit Vincent; that man was purer than a saint. His eyes darted to the man who had attacked him, and Finnick charged.

It didn't take long for the four men that started the fire to lie unconscious on the ground. But the homeless, angry, and intoxicated individuals around the area took the fight as a sign to start brawling amongst themselves.

"Someone started a good party now, haven't they, Vinny?" Finnick asked and helped the man to his feet.

"You call this a party?" he asked.

"Add a good pint and a pretty woman, and we have a feast. Stay close to me, Vinny; I will watch your back," Finnick said calmly.

"Hey, O'Malley!" Manny yelled and before Finnick could turn, Manny sucker-punched him in the face.

When Finnick fell, Patrick roared. The fire was almost out, thanks to all the helpful hands, but the smoke was still extremely thick.

Patrick was covered in ash when he appeared by his brother's side. Rather than check on Finnick, his body slammed into Manny, tackling him down to the ground.

"You ugly, stupid son of a bitch!" Manny roared as the two of them rolled around on the ground.

"If you want to see someone ugly, look into the mirror," Patrick hollered.

"You stupid fucking man! Why couldn't you be a god damn gentleman!" Manny yelled as they rolled right onto the feet of a squad of police officers.

At the sight of the law enforcement, people scattered in the opposite direction. No one had the money for bail, and the government would use any excuse to send them to prison. They now had Manny and Patrick. Finnick slowly stood and wiped off the blood from his face, watching his brother.

"Don't do anything stupid," Conner whispered from behind him.

"I am not an idiot," Finnick said.

"That is debatable."

Conner had been driving and saw the fight. He knew that

getting involved would cost him and Porter, but with the store covered

in smoke, he had no choice. Not once did Conner raise a hand and join the festivities; instead, he made sure that the O'Malley boys went willingly, and surprisingly Vincent, was cuffed as well. This was not how anyone pictured their night would end.

CHAPTER SEVEN

Two days. Two long and grueling days those four men sat in a cramped cell. Pissing and shitting into a bucket that no one wanted to be nearby. Battered, bruised, and exhausted, they wanted nothing more than to get out of there, but the charges were read.

Regardless of how the fight started, they were each charged with fighting in a public place, being under the influence of a contraband substance, and whatever else the arresting officer thought up. It was all an excuse, a reach that the detectives were using to keep these four individuals locked up.

"I want to get out of here!" a man in another cell shouted.

"Shut the fuck up! Some of us are trying to sleep!" another hollered.

"Hey, kid, what is your name?" Conner asked Vincent, who looked terrified.

Vincent probably had a few broken fingers from the way he was holding his hand. No one gave him a chance to explain; why would they? They associated the poor bastard with gang-related violence, no chance to defend himself. He had every right to be scared.

"Nobody cares!" a woman spat and was ready to scream

some more, until she saw Conner's face.

Porter was not to be messed with; everyone knew that. Even if his men were locked up, they were still under his protection. One that sadly extended to the fourth person in their little jailhouse party.

"Vincent," he whispered.

"You did a brave thing, Vincent, sticking up for the block. We will never forget that" Conner said as Detective Colins leaned up against the bars, looking at the four before him.

"You should not have gotten involved," the detective said to Conner.

"Wasn't going to let the store burn. It is not only the O'Malleys but the entire community's. What should I have done?" he asked in a smug, no-bullshit expression.

Colins knew all about what happened that night. Looking at the men before him, they made sure whoever was responsible for the fire was beaten and good as dead. But it wasn't that simple. Whoever was behind this made it so no evidence was found. They only had eyewitness testimony to go on, and that wasn't as reliable as Colins wanted it to be.

"Kept on driving. I made sure the car was taken care of, so they didn't take it, but they insist that the four of you stand trial," Detective Colins explained.

"For what?" Conner asked as the other three men actively listened to the conversation.

"Disturbing the peace, endangerment of minors, public fighting, and intoxication. The intoxication won't stick because they have no proof, but the others, it is hard to pick out who really was involved or not. It will take some time, which they will drag out."

"Bail?"

"Porter refused. Said you need to learn a lesson."

"Figures…" Patrick mumbled, and his brother hit him hard.

"Don't be rude," Finnick snapped.

"Look, boys, I will make sure you get out of here. The trial is hogwash, we all know it, but you will have to serve your time in here. All of you," Colins explained as his eyes found Vincent.

The man had been quiet, minus the few answers he seemed to squeak out of his tiny body. What possessed him to do it? He must have known the moment he got involved something like this would happen, but when Finnick stood, he walked over to the bars and looked to the detective.

"Have you heard anything about the shop?" Finnick inquired.

"Your fight didn't help anything, but the quick action you boys took did save it. The windows are boarded up, and your pop is getting the community to help with the inside damages. You all were lucky. Any idea who you pissed off?" the detective asked as Patrick scoffed at the question.

"Who didn't we piss off…" Finnick said, and it sadly did not help.

They aggravated enough people to make the list too long to make an assumption. Everyone knew that Daniels was behind it, but they had no proof and he never acted without an agenda. Someone put the idea in his mind, and that person was the real perpetrator behind it all.

"What is the word on the street?" Conner asked.

"We all know who did the hit, but like always, there is no proof to link him to the crime. I will keep you posted. All I am asking is you keep your noses clean until you are released," Colins said and backed away from the bars.

"Any tips?"

"Keep looking mad, no one wants to piss your boss off, so they will leave you well enough alone," Detective Colins replied and walked out of sight.

Once again, the four of them were alone with their thoughts. All they did the past two days was think but they all looked to the bars when they heard heels and were shocked to see Linda Bishop.

"Please tell me you are all right?" Linda said as Patrick, Finnick, and Vincent all looked at Conner, who the woman was peering at with longing and fear.

He walked the few steps to the cell bars and reached through. His hands held dried blood and dirt, but she did not seem to mind. All that mattered was to feel him, to see for herself that Conner was okay. He gently put his soiled hand on her cheek and stroked it.

The look of love was all over his face, a look that no one ever saw past that ugly mug.

"I am all right, but you shouldn't be here," he said softly as she started to cry.

"It isn't fair. Everyone is talking about how the hooded men started the fire and how you were only making sure the brothers did not cause trouble. Never once did you raise your hand; that is not anyone's blood but Patrick's. You did nothing wrong; you shouldn't be in here." She wept as tears stained her lovely pink dress.

"Listen to me, my sweet one, I will get out of here…" he informed her as a deputy walked up.

"You're free to go, Mr. McDonald," the deputy said as a look of confusion spread across everyone's face.

"Is this a trick?" he asked.

"This lovely lady posted your bail. You will be informed of your court date," the deputy explained as Linda ran into his arms the moment Conner took a step forward.

No one knew anything about the man. All that he presented was a bad ass individual who did not allow anyone to get close. That is what made him so valuable to Porter; no one could get to him or have

any leverage. But with the way he held Linda, that theory was tossed right out the window.

"I would appreciate if the three of you kept this quiet. I do not want anyone to hurt her," Conner said to the men in the cell.

"Sure, like anyone would believe us," Patrick said with a nod, knowing he would keep the man's secret.

"Damn. That man has all the luck," Finnick muttered.

When the deputy did not leave and the door was still open, everyone was silent. He did not let anyone out, but when the brothers looked to Vincent, it seemed the deputy was waiting for him.

"You too, Vincent," the deputy said.

Vincent looked confused but did not question it. He did not want to be here any longer than he had to. It was not that he feared the brothers; it was the reputation that could be troublesome to him. He had to stay quiet, almost invisible.

"Not the two of you," the deputy spat and slammed the door.

It was a mistake, Finnick knew that when he attacked them, but no one dared hurt their pop or his store. That store was their father's dream, his way of providing when they were boys. Those two would do anything to make sure that shop was protected. Which is the reason they got into the business with Porter to begin with. He needed muscle, and they needed cash.

"Who do you think did it?" Patrick asked his brother, now that the two of them were alone.

"I do not even know where to begin, Pat, between the city wanting everyone to conform to the new rules of the block to whoever opposes Porter. There is no way to narrow it down,"

Finnick explained.

"Gasoline isn't cheap. They were using it to make those fire balls like it was water. Which means money is involved. We all know

Daniels would not use his own funds for his educational moments," Patrick said.

"Which leaves out Lawrence Murphy," Finnick muttered as they both laughed.

They both heard about what Porter did to scare the man. No one dared go toe-to-toe with Porter in his city, and nobody tried, until Lawrence fucking Murphy. Porter needed to make an example, and sadly, Lawrence would be that example. But their laughter died as soon as Patrick spoke.

"Porter wouldn't betray us. We never made him angry…" Patrick murmured.

"He wouldn't do it to us. The only way we can know who attacked the store is to go after Daniels," Finnick added as his brother tackled him.

"Watch your goddamn mouth, Brother. If anyone hears you want to go after Daniels, that is like inviting Death himself to your doorstep. We will not borrow trouble. Once we are let out of here, we will ask Porter for help," Patrick responded and slowly let his brother go.

"He needs to be taken care of. For everyone's sake, not just ours," Finnick said quietly to his brother.

"I know, but Daniels has eyes everywhere. He would know if someone was after him in a heartbeat." Both men frowned.

The brothers had to be careful. Even in here, they were being

watched. If the wrong thing was said or the right person saw something they did not like, it could mean their death.

It was not a war on crime and alcohol; it was a war on everyone who was not born in America. Some wanted any excuse to have them killed. Both of the brothers read about the Salem Witch Trials,

who said they wouldn't change their targets to good ole Irishmen?

CHAPTER EIGHT

The brothers were stuck in that cell for two weeks. No one cared that they were there. Someone must have forgotten to care for them because they really started to smell. Like Conner and Detective Colins had instructed, both men kept their nose clean and caught no trouble.

Because of their willingness and cooperation, they were let out with a warning. But the punishment they received at home was one they would never talk about. Patrick and Finnick made sure to always have a smile on their faces when they were working the store, and today was no different.

"You two won't be getting into any more fights now, will you?" a woman asked at the register while Finnick looked as innocent as possible.

"I promise you, Mrs. Townsend, my boys learned their lesson," the O'Malleys' father said sternly.

"It is such a shame about what happened. I am glad everyone is all right," the woman said as Finnick stood there, not able to get away.

"The store looks good as new," another added as the boys' father nodded.

"The community really came together to help me out. I could not have reopened so quickly without them."

"Oh, my dear Patrick, look how filthy you are." Mrs. Townsend gasped the moment Patrick walked into the store after a delivery.

"Would you like a hug, Mrs. Townsend?" Patrick asked as he opened his arms.

They were a flirt to all the older women. It was what made many of them come here over a store closer to home. The brothers were not oblivious to their looks and enjoyed giving the attention the older women seemed to need. When the bell rang, they both looked up to the most beautiful being they had ever seen.

"Good morning, Ms. Mitchell," Finnick said as he was at her side within moments.

It was common for people to have a mixed reaction for Cameron Mitchell. Even though she was born here in America and her father worked with the postal service, she had gotten some backlash because of her mother's lineage. But damn, she was beautiful.

"Good morning. I was wondering if you could help me," Cameron said and handed Finnick her list.

"Of course."

It was then Finnick realized what he had done. Because he had approached her first, he had to step away and do the job. As he internally groaned at his oversight, he turned and headed towards the shelf behind the counter. Then Patrick walked over with a grin on his face.

"How have you been?" Patrick asked as he tripped on his own untied shoes and caught himself on the beam in the middle of the store.

That action put poor Cameron between him and the beam. They were now only an inch apart, and the way his body engulfed her very existence caused Cameron to form a clever smile on her face. She had been with many men, she was not a virgin to say the least, but when Sarah Monroe walked in, she interrupted the intense moment.

"It is nice to see you are out of jail, Patrick O'Malley," Sarah scolded as Carmen could not help but laugh.

"I did hear about the two of you being thrown into a cell over a fight," she added, and Patrick glared at Sarah.

"Poor timing," he whispered.

"I am aware," Sarah replied, keeping a smile on her face.

Everyone thought she was so innocent because of her plain looks and job. She was always proper in public, and that made her clever. No one suspected a schoolteacher would be the accountant for Porter. She was the one who held all the money, the numbers, and knew where it was all stored. She also had some mathematical skills that made her an excellent asset at the poker tables.

"I am glad the two of you are not hurt. I do not know what your father would have done if something happened," Sarah said, and

Cameron took the moment the two of them were talking to walk over to Linda, who looked confused.

"Stop it," Patrick hissed under his breath.

"I am well aware of what I am doing."

"And what exactly do you think you're doing?"

"Saving poor Cameron from the likes of you. You're welcome."

"You, okay?" Cameron asked Linda as she held up two jars.

"I was told to get two-quart size canning jars for tomatoes, but I have only ever done jam. Do I need caps? And the rubber? We used a piece of cloth for the cover when I was a little girl," Linda said in a panic.

"Well, I am not one with numbers, darling, but let me get someone over here who needs to escape a grumpy Irishman. Sarah!"

"Keep that nose of yours clean or else," Sarah threatened as a smile returned before walking over to Cameron and Linda.

"I need help badly," Linda explained as Sarah looked up to Cameron for clarification.

"How many tomatoes do you need to can?" Cameron asked as Linda counted on her fingers.

This was the one thing Linda needed to do to show her uncle she could do something without his help. If there was ever any hope that she could be with Conner, she needed to learn how to do things on her own.

"How many tomatoes do you have?" Sarah asked in a calm

tone, the ones she used for her students.

"I have three plants and I picked seventeen tomatoes from them," Linda replied.

"Are they big and can fit in your hand? Or tiny like grapes?" Sarah asked as Patrick now stood behind them, listening to the math lesson unfold.

"Big."

"The average weight of a large tomato is around twelve to sixteen ounces. Depending on the size variance, let us call it twenty ounces. You have about three hundred and forty ounces worth of tomatoes, and with extra variable, it is safe to lock in that number.

That will round your number of needed cans to about ten and a half, but let us call it eleven. It will be safe to have at least one extra in case you break one; never be too careful. And the price, I am always

looking for a good sale, so it is cheaper if you buy the dozen boxed over individually."

"What is the difference?" Linda asked as Cameron chuckled.

As she did the math quickly in her head, that smile never left her face. Numbers were safe for Sarah, she loved them, and she always knew what to expect.

"At ninety cents a box, that makes each jar seven and a half cents. If you buy them individually, they are marked up to nine cents. That is a difference of ninety cents for the box or a dollar and eight cents for the individuals. I also recommended the jar caps;

they keep them preserved long periods of time. There is a one and three-quarters cent mark up; I can do the math," Sarah said as Linda waved her hands.

"No, thank you, I understand. I am getting used to making these decisions for myself and realizing how horrible I am. Thank you, though, for all your help," Linda said as Sarah brushed off the thanks.

"I am going to give my list to Patrick, so you two have fun." Linda said walked away.

"Impressive," Cameron said.

"I know." Sarah replied.

There were so many people in the store that no one noticed the two of them escape. When Patrick moved his mouth to speak, she hit him hard across the face.

"Listen to me very carefully, Patrick," Sarah said as her tone changed drastically. "We lost thousands of dollars the two weeks you and Finnick were locked up. Keep your nose clean, and if you start another fight, I will personally request Porter find your replacement."

No one saw this side of her, the hardworking woman who refused anything other than perfection. Porter made sure her secret life was protected, so taking off her mask in the open was risky.

"Stay away from Cameron; she is innocent," he said as Sarah laughed.

"After all I said, your body is still being controlled by your dick?" she snapped, and he gave her a hard look.

"I am serious."

"No one is innocent, good sir. Look around. We are all in the belly of the beast and are along for the ride. Do not screw up!" Sarah yelled, and her thought process was cut short when she heard screaming outside.

They both followed the hurried footsteps out of the store, and everyone had to take a step back from the terrible sight before them. Fire. The flames were massive, coming out of every window and door. The smoke filled the entire block. It was the butcher shop, and it was engulfed in a burning inferno.

"Where are the authorities?" someone yelled as many people started a line from other places to get water to the scolding flames.

"Keep the children away!" a woman shouted.

Families lived above that shop. Many of those families had children. When Cameron heard a child's scream, she ran forward. Never did she jump into the middle of any problem, she knew better than to get too close, but no one else seemed to react to the cry.

"Cameron!" Patrick yelled and pulled her back.

"I need to get that boy!"

"We will get them."

Falling debris littered the streets and sky. It was Patrick who watched as Cameron's skirt suddenly took ablaze. There was no thinking; Patrick knelt and ripped it off.

"Oh my god!" she yelled in a panic at Patrick's action, and when she saw it was on fire, she screamed.

As Patrick was trying to put out the fire, Finnick picked up Cameron quickly, not wanting her to be embarrassed now that her bare legs were showing. Both brothers came to her aid and turned their back to the flames taking over the store.

The welts already started to form. They covered Cameron's legs. She did not cry. One good scream was all she gave, but now, it was only a whimper. Her hands held onto him tightly. Finnick was her protector, and Cameron was relying on his strength. She had to believe she wasn't going to die.

When Finnick made it up the stairs, he gently put her down on the sofa. All the pillows and blankets were pushed away; he did not want anything to touch her. Finnick tried so hard not to panic.

"It hurts," she whimpered as Linda appeared with Sarah right behind her.

"Get the doctor!" Finnick hollered as Sarah moved without question.

"I do not know much about burns," Linda said, but Finnick stood quickly and walked to another open part of the room.

Linda watched as Finnick pushed aside a table and pulled up the rug. It was not unheard of to have secret compartments, but this compartment held all their money that the brothers slowly gave back to their father's business. Along with the money, unopened bottles of whiskey greeted him as the man reached in. When

Finnick produced the bottle with a familiar label, he rushed it over to Cameron.

"Drink this. It will dull the pain until the doctor gets here," he instructed.

Cameron didn't think twice about the command; she took that bottle into her hand and brought it to her lips. How she drank it showed this wasn't her first time with the illegal substance. She chugged almost

half the bottle before Sarah came running back with a tired doctor in tow.

"I got him," Sarah announced.

The doctor paused to look around the room before immediately going to Cameron's side and getting to work. She screamed when he applied the cool cloth after he took all the debris off her wounds. Her stockings were stripped, and thankfully, she passed out so he could finish. Three hours later, the Doctor looked grim as she slept.

"She needs to stay off those legs. Change the bandages as often as you can and make sure they are clean. Her body needs to fight the infection. I will make sure she has everything she needs and inform her father."

"How much?" Patrick asked.

"The debt is between her father and me, but you boys saved her life. That knowledge will make it so, your little stunt in jail will be easier to forgive," he said and tipped his hat before leaving.

They were lucky. A few weeks ago, their own store was a victim of a fire, but the quick action made it so it stayed standing, but the butcher shop, there was no saving it. Many people relied on the butcher shop, which was now ash. It was not only a place for food but also for employment. Two fires so close did not make it an accident. It was set deliberately, and it was all anyone could talk about.

CHAPTER NINE

"Those fires, people won't shut up about them. Four fucking weeks of nothing but those damn fires." Lawrence mumbled as he looked out of Connie's window to all the people down below.

"Four people died in the butcher shop fire, Lawrence, and the O'Malley brothers were thrown in jail over the fire at their father's store. It is serious. Someone is setting them up," Connie said.

Lawrence had not left her apartment for weeks. He owed so much in back rent that the landlord finally kicked him out. Of course, he would stay with her, but the complaining about everything and using her place to hide was starting to get to her.

"Regardless, I cannot draw any more attention to myself. My whole idea has blown up in my face, and I need cash. Do you have any?" Lawrence asked and looked to Connie.

She wanted to be surprised, but Connie loved him too much to pretend to be shocked. There was no working electricity in her apartment or running water; she, too, was behind on her payments and every cent she made at Porter's club went straight into Lawrence's pocket. He bled her dry, and when she did not answer, Lawrence sighed.

When he looked back outside, Lawrence caught sight of Senator Hamilton Murphy and got angry all over again. That man was loaded and flaunted it with his golden pocket watch, new shoes, and that stupid hat. Everyone flocked to him with questions and sought encouragement. Everyone supported him, the rumors of his presidency run were circulating, but the sour taste of Hamilton's rejection was still raw and he wanted to show his brother of circumstance he could not hide from their past.

"Senator Murphy!" a reporter yelled as Hamilton shook a few hands of the people who approached him.

As he turned to face the reporter, that fake smile was plastered ear to ear. It was then he realized he was only a few buildings away from the clothing store. A store that he knew about all too well. There was a hint of longing in his eyes. He loved Vincent. There was no mistaking that fact. When they were together, it was the most magical moment. Vincent understood him, listened to him, and was encouraging in ways no one else was.

He needed that closeness, wanted that companionship but it was the image of a straight man he needed to keep. Those eyes went from the store to the reporter who was already asking questions. So many questions, and no matter what answer he gave, it was never good enough for anyone.

"Senator Murphy, what do you have to say regarding the most recent string of arson cases in this neighborhood?" the reporter asked, ready to take down his answers with his pencil and notebook.

"This neighborhood is a cornerstone for the Irish community. Every business was built from the ground up by families who left horrible situations to give their children better lives. The grocery store

and butcher shop are loved and will continue to be loved. I will make sure to personally take interest in finding the culprits involved who not only took innocent lives but also destroyed hardworking families' dreams."

—

"Hard working my ass. Nobody works harder than me," Betty spat, hearing the interview with Senator Murphy.

Her hair was matted, clothing wrinkled. Never once had anyone seen her not looking haggard and disappointed in her very existence. The fire was the only thing anyone was talking about, and Betty knew better; she knew who did it. Of course, she would never tell, not unless someone paid her more than her life was worth.

Betty looked up to the balcony above the alley and saw a familiar individual, a man who was freed from prison only after two days. Even though all the talk was regarding the fires, a few simple whispers spoke of a woman. Conner's woman. Never had he had a person in his life who could be used against him.

Betty smirked. She knew full well that this little piece of information would come in handy someday to someone who would pay handsomely for it.

—

"Talk to me," Conner whispered as he sat on a terrace, overlooking the city below.

His focus was not on the noise outside but on the woman lying in his bed. Conner woke up too early in the morning; years of early morning runs made it so he always got up before the sun rose. But his Linda, on his bed, under his blanket, was his happiness, his light in

this very mysterious world.

"Come here…" she whispered and outreached her arm.

God, she was beautiful. Hair as bright as the sun and curly, down past her shoulders. Those blue eyes like water looked towards him and they both smiled. Never did that man smile.

He was in love, a word he used to laugh at others for saying. But this feeling, this ache in his chest, Conner knew it was for her. As he slowly stood and walked over to the bare woman in his bed, he could not help but feel a need to take her.

Conner smiled, gently pulling the blanket away so that he could see her body. Linda had the most contagious smile, and when Conner leaned down to kiss her, she met him halfway, wrapping her arms around his neck.

"Come back to bed," she whined, pulling him closer.

Laughter escaped Conner's lips. For someone who had been through a dark and mudded past, laughter was one thing he would never have. Happiness. Love. Contentment. It was all here with her, and he would do anything to make her his forever.

"You seem troubled," Linda whispered, snuggling close to her beloved.

"How can you tell?" he teased.

"For one, your brow has tension lines," Linda started as Conner laughed once more.

That laughter caused a playful smack to come against his clothed chest. When he leaned in to kiss her, Conner entangled his fingers in hers. He wanted to capture this woman, now and forever.

"Second," Linda continued, "your shoulders are rigid, and you're distracted. What can I do to ease your burden?"

God, Conner loved this woman. She was always looking out for him, making sure he was taken care of. Conner never had that before, and he would never let it go, no matter what happened.

"I love you," Conner whispered.

"I love you, too," Linda said, slowly unbuttoning his shirt with that ambition in her eyes that Conner could never say no to.

—

When one man was spending the morning with his love, others were trying to solve the unsolvable. The O'Malley brothers owed Porter everything. He not only gave them employment but also made it his mission to make all businesses in the community successful.

"I do not know what more I can do for your father," Porter said to the brothers who found him at the most inconvenient time.

During the day, he was dealing with issues all over the city. Between the speakeasies, the community, and the demons of City Hall, he had no time for himself. But when the brothers approached him, rather than turn them away, he was a listening ear. At least until he got too annoyed.

"I know you have already done enough, Porter," Finnick said while Patrick agreed.

"It isn't enough to put your mind at ease. For that, I am sorry boys. We are doing all we can to figure out who torched your place and the butcher shop. So far, we are coming up with no leads."

The money for the windows, to replace the burned boards, and to order new product, it was all out of Porter's pocket. Never had the man asked for anything in return, but the brothers knew that they owed him. It was not about the money; it was about respect.

"We have a run in two weeks. I want you both on it," Porter said to the two men.

When Porter stood, the empty bar was getting cleaned up and ready for tomorrow's opening. Sadly, this location could not be open every night. Porter needed to move to avoid suspicion, but when his city was attacked, it did not sit well with him.

"Boss, the detective is here," a man informed Porter who nodded, watching the brothers leave the room,

"Be honest with me, Porter. How far are you willing to go?" Detective Colins asked as he pulled up a new chair to the table and sat right next to his friend.

Porter had a cigarette in his hand as the smoke rose between the two of them. There was silence, the only sound was the mopping in the background, but when Porter took a puff, he finally looked to his friend.

"I need something on Daniels, something I can use," Porter said as Colins leaned back in his chair, taking out his own carton of cigarettes.

"If I get caught following him, it will risk your protection," Colins said, lighting a match.

"I am aware of the risk."

"I am reminding you."

"Any family?"

"Nope."

"Lovers?"

"Everyone uses a whore. Betty Tyler will be costly, and it goes both ways. We don't know how deep Daniels's reach goes. I can't ask around City Hall."

"I know…" Porter whispered as both men fell silent.

The long eerie silence was dreaded. There was no solution to this mess. Daniels got away with everything because he was untouchable. His relationship with the city officials made his face known, and he would be missed if he disappeared. Killing him was out.

His contacts. No one knew how Daniels got individuals to do the deeds, but they were never found. Those four men who attacked the O'Malley store were still missing. There was no evidence, pictures, or witnesses. It was like they were never there.

"Be honest with me, Ben, how deep?" Porter finally asked, putting out his cigarette.

"More than you already are?" Colins teased.

The glare from Porter only caused Colins to laugh. They needed to laugh to stay sane. Both men chuckled until it slowly died like any happiness they ever felt.

"Don't worry about it, Port. I'll watch your back."

"I can take care of myself."

"I know, but I still have your back," Colins whispered and stood. He had a job to do and if he took longer than a few moments here, it would be reported.

—

That night was not quiet for everyone. Gretchen demanded to speak to her brother. Now that he was in Porter's crew, it was impossible to track him down. But that night he allowed her to find him, in an alley near City Hall.

"Did you do something?" Gretchen demanded.

Everyone was talking about the fires, speculating on who was doing it. Gretchen felt awful, felt like it was all her fault. She was angry and, in her anger, begged her brother to do something. Now that she

was levelheaded, she felt like this was all her fault.

"What are you harping about?" Manny demanded, grabbing her arm.

She was hysterical. Gretchen always was dramatic and emotional. First, she wanted one thing, demanded it, begged for it. Then the next day, she changed her mind. Manny could not keep up, which was why she needed a keeper, someone to take care of her and make sure she was doing things that were in her best interest.

"The grocery—" she started, but Manny covered her mouth.

"Shut your mouth!" he barked and pushed her up against the wall.

Her eyes widened at her brother's roughness. Gretchen knew

that he only wanted what was best for her, but she had this feeling, this guilt that it was all her fault. She knew, as did everyone in the city that Manny rode with Porter. He had a reputation that many feared. Was Porter the one who started the fires? Why would he do such a thing?

"You will never speak of it again. Stop thinking. Do you hear me?" Manny spat and did not remove his hand until Gretchen nodded.

Her brother used to be kind. He always looked out for her when they were kids, but ever since he started to run with Porter, he became cold and mean. Gretchen was seeing it now; it was all Porter's fault.

CHAPTER TEN

"This goddamn rain is not letting up!" Patrick yelled.

It had been raining nonstop for the past three days. The boys were driving in this destructive weather with no hope of it letting up. Twice they had to dig themselves out and with their cargo, the truck was heavier than it should have been.

"I can see that, Mr. Weatherman!" Finnick yelled back.

"Go fuck yourself!"

"Make me!"

The visibility was even worse. It was a downpour. Already they were late picking up the cargo. Now the delivery was looking to be late as well. They had two weeks to prepare for this run, but the rain, was something they did not account for. They should have accounted for all weather, a mistake on their part.

"God damn it..." Patrick muttered as he slowly took his foot off the gas.

A fallen tree. When the truck came to a full stop, the brothers mumbled their hate for the rain and pulled up the hoods on their jackets. It was always a two-man job, which was why they went everywhere together, but moving that tree, would take much more than two people.

"If we go back, we will hit the city after daylight and bring unneeded attention," Finnick observed, and Patrick hit him hard.

"No shit!" Patrick yelled and walked back towards the truck.

"What do you want to do?"

"We need to move that damn log and keep going!" When Patrick reached the truck, the passenger door was closed.

He knew Finnick had left it open. The one thing his brother was known for was leaving things open, but what he saw in the window was the barrel of a shotgun. Seconds. Patrick had seconds to hit the ground to avoid a shell to the face. Bang.

Broken glass littered the ground at his side as the sound of the blast alerted Finnick. The moment his brother turned around; the truck was surrounded by masked individuals all holding shotguns. Rain poured down from the darkened sky, but Patrick grabbed one of their legs and pulled him down.

"A little help here!" Patrick yelled towards his brother.

"You got this?" Finnick asked but was already on his way over, itching for a fight.

"Of course, I do. Didn't want you missing all the fun."

There were seven men. Two surrounded Patrick as he was wrestling with the one he had pulled down. Four were on the other side of the truck, waiting for Finnick to play. Once the massive man came over, fists started flying. If they wanted a fight, they got one.

"Miss me?" Finnick yelled and punched someone else.

Each man was armed. Even the brothers had a side piece, but everyone chose their fists. Patrick and the three men at his side were all rolling around in the mud. The truck was a barrier, one that they used to their advantage.

"How come you only have three?" Finnick teased and threw one man against the truck as it rocked back and forth.

"You said you could win anything. Prove it!" Patrick yelled and shoved one aside.

"Don't want your ego to get too big," Finnick called out.

Lights flashed in the distance. Red and blue. Those lights got closer, and when the brothers noticed, they both swore.

"Fuck it, run!" Patrick called out.

They both immediately got up and ran into the woods. They could not get caught again. Regardless if the shipment was lost, if they got arrested, they would never see the outside of the jail cell, and their father, along with Porter, would murder them.

—

The once-empty road was now filled with people. Law enforcement littered the whole area. Thankfully, the rain was covering their tracks, but the truck was still in plain sight. How they knew the brothers would be there was a question for another time, but right now, the O'Malleys needed to disappear.

"What do we have?" the sheriff called out as he drove up to the scene.

"An empty truck. Whatever they were carrying is long gone," a deputy said, but the sheriff looked up to see a man walking towards them.

His shoes were covered in mud, and the rain was pouring over his hat and jacket. The way he moved, though, was not directly towards the truck. No. His attention was towards the tree line.

"Who is that?" the sheriff asked.

Everyone turned to watch the stranger. The man walked around the perimeter, focusing on his feet. Tracks were everywhere, slowly being drowned out by the heavy rainfall. They could be from the ones who owned the vehicle or from the countless others walking around. This whole crime scene was a mess.

"A prohis...one of those prohibition federal agents from Washington," the deputy replied as the man bent down to pick something up.

"I will not have a federal agent steal my case. We both know that this is Porter's truck. This arrest will be huge," the sheriff snapped as the agent walked towards them.

The agent had a jacket in his hand. He held it out to the side as if it were dangerous. It dripped with mud and water. The jacket made a loud slush when he plopped it on the back of the truck and started searching its pockets.

"Look," the sheriff tried to say when he hastily approached the man.

The agent did not acknowledge the sheriff, not right away. He pulled a card out of the jacket pocket and held it up. Everyone went silent. His dark eyes looked at the card and frowned. The hat he wore covered the bright red hair that grouped him into a crowd that was currently suffering. The agent lived through that suffering, knew what alcohol could do to a family, so when he saw the name Detective Benjamin Colins on the card, he knew exactly what to do.

The sheriff could not get a word out to the agent. He was there one minute and gone the next. He never said a word to anyone, and that card was all he needed. The pieces were slowly falling into place.

CHAPTER ELEVEN

A loud knock on the door was barely heard over the rainfall. While the whole investigation was going on regarding the truck, Benjamin Colins was pacing back and forth at home because he had not seen Linda today. There was no note at home he could find, one to tell him where she was. He was worried. She had never been gone this long before.

Back and forth. His shoes pattered on the floor, but he stopped, the moment he heard the loud knock on the door. He ignored it at first, too wrapped up in his thoughts, but when they did not go away, Colins grabbed his service revolver and stalked to the door.

"What do you want?" he snapped the moment he opened the door but was surprised to see uniformed officers greeting him.

"I am sorry we have to do this, Ben, but you need to come with us," one of the officers said.

"What is this about?" he asked.

"Please Detective Colins, do not make a scene," the other said as Colins frowned but took a step back.

He needed to find Linda. She had not been home or told him about what was going on in her life. There was something she was hiding. He placed his revolver on the table and held up his hands. He knew these two officers, and thankfully, they did not put him in cuffs. None of his neighbors would know he was a suspect; all they would think was he was going to help solve a case.

Now, he was sitting in a room, one that he had been in many times but never on this side of the table. This was madness, he had done nothing wrong, but in seeing a new face walk in, he knew the whole situation was shifting.

Hair of fire. Like all the Irish folks who lived in the city, but he was not from Boston. Colins knew everyone; this was a new face. There was a silence as the stranger walked in, his suit sharp and polished, and his shoes matched and well-kept. Even the hat in his hand was brand new.

"Thank you for coming all this way, Detective Colins. I am Federal Agent Marcus Willard; I have been asked to come to Boston from Washington to assist in the crime that has arisen due to that lovely Eighteenth Amendment we all hear about." Colins leaned back and crossed his arms.

"That is all fine and dandy. Do you mind telling me why I was taken from my home and brought here like a fugitive? I know my rights, and a few were violated in not telling me why I am under arrest," Colins said as Willard smirked.

"You and I are going to have a little chat about that card on the table. The card that has your name on it," Willard commented as

Colins looked to the muddy, drying business card that was indeed his own.

"And? I give those out all the time," Colins replied.

"Indeed, you do, and it would not be the first time a criminal would have it on them.

 I read your record; you try to keep your nose clean but always seem to be at the right place, at the wrong time." Willard sat down across from Colins.

They both fell silent once more, staring each other down. Colins was not under arrest, they could not take away his pistol or badge, but when Willard reached down, he pulled up an overflowing folder that was not identified on the outside.

"You have been on the force for twelve years, and your record isn't exactly sparkling." Willard opened the folder.

"What are you really after, Willard?"

"You grew up on the streets, parents were alcoholics, and it was a miracle you survived long enough to make it into the police academy. Unfortunately, it does not matter what you did as a child. If there were no major crimes, you could hold a badge," Willard explained as Colins laughed.

"You can hold me at most for three days. Are we going to have a sleepover, or are we done?"

Colins's harsh tone did not phase Willard, but when he held up a photograph, Colins calmed down. It was of a group of schoolchildren standing in front of a school building with smiles on their faces. Willard put the picture on the table next to the card and pointed to two boys in the front.

"This is you, Benjamin Colins, and that little boy beside you, is what the streets like to call Porter, but his real name is Emmet Colins, your foster brother."

"Em and I moving together doesn't make us friends," Colins explained as Willard pulled out

another photo.

It was of two adults in coffins leaning up against a brick wall. It was taken right before they were buried. Those two people were Colins's parents, who were killed in a car accident because they were under the influence. He was only three years old when they died.

"I know you understand firsthand what alcohol can do to a family. Which is why these accusations of you helping Porter baffles me. You are the poster boy of Prohibition. Families do not want to end up broken, their children having to be taken care of by strangers, yet here you are, your card at a transportation raid. It raises a lot of questions," Willard said as Colins slowly stood and adjusted his jacket.

"When you are ready for some real charges, you know where to find me." Colins walked out of the office.

Benjamin was angry. Not only at himself but also at the damn O'Malley brothers for leaving his card at the scene. It was no secret Porter had police protection, but no one had ever come after Colins before; he was too rooted in the department. But now, with this outside force, they could all be in trouble.

"Going somewhere?" Willard called out as Colins made it only a few steps before he was surrounded.

"What are my charges?" Benjamin asked.

"Detective Benjamin Colins, you are under arrest for the violation of the Eighteenth Amendment. That falls under the transportation of illegal substances over state and county borders. You have a niece, don't you? We will make sure she is notified," Willard stated as Colins did not say a word. He looked to his captain and knew he was in deep trouble.

CHAPTER TWELVE

"Tell me what happened, Cameron," Sarah said as she tried to soothe the woman who had been crying ever since she arrived at the hospital.

"I do not know. One moment he was fine and then the next he was on the floor," Cameron said between sobs.

"You were at the store?"

"I was picking up a few pounds of flour. I was going to bake the O'Malley boys a cake for rescuing me. My legs still hurt, but I needed to get out of my apartment. When I got there, he was fine, Sarah. All he had was a little cough."

Sarah let out a sigh and looked around her. The hospital was filled like always with the sick and dying. It was never a place anyone wanted to be unless they had to, but Cameron refused to leave; she did not want to leave the boy's father alone.

They didn't know that a few rooms away Connie sat on a bed. Her facial expression was distant as she looked out the open window.

The bruises on her body and cuts on her face told a story, one that if she thought about, the tears would start.

Connie would not cry out loud, not like Cameron; she would cry within herself, all alone. She loved Lawrence, wanted to be with him, but the man he had become; was one that she no longer knew. In the reflection of the window, she thought she saw Porter, but when Connie turned to look at the open doorway, no one was there.

"Then what happened?" Sarah asked, trying to calm Cameron down.

"He kept on coughing. It got harder and harder for him to breathe."

"The brothers?" Sarah asked, but Cameron let out a whole new line of sobs.

"I don't know! They should be here. There was blood. It was coming out of his mouth every time he coughed. Blood!" she yelled as Sarah sighed but jumped when she felt a hand on her shoulder.

Sarah immediately turned to see Porter. He covered her mouth to muffle the scream but quickly removed it to not cause a scene. Cameron's sobs covered the noise of Sarah walking away. They both walked into an empty patient room, and Porter closed the door, his expression serious.

"How is he?" Porter inquired.

"Tuberculosis. Not looking good. Are they keeping their heads down?" Sarah asked, and Porter handed her a small notebook.

"I need all the receipts added and the damage known. With the prohis in the city, it is harder to transport."

"Did you tell them?"

"If I do, they will leave the safe house and be at his side. It is too risky."

"Leaving them in the dark will risk them bailing on you. Can you trust them to play it cool now that we have new players in town?"

"Don't question me, Sarah!"

"It is my job to question you!" Sarah yelled.

She was the money. Porter knew better than to make the money angry. When a few people walked by the door, he dodged to the side so that he could not be seen. They had to be careful; this Agent Willard had been looking for him. Thankfully, he did not have anything on him yet, but the questioning was the start of the downfall.

"You really are worried about the agent, aren't you?" Sarah observed and Porter opened the door, not answering her.

Cameron continued to cry. She felt responsible for something that was uncontrollable. The sickness was not as deadly, now that personal hygiene had improved, but if the boys lost their father, they would lose what grounded them. That was why Porter did not tell them their father was in the hospital. He needed them because Porter got word that Colins had been arrested and officially charged with aiding him.

—

"I cannot believe you are doing this, Colins. After all we did for you." the captain said.

So many of his coworkers had come by his jail cell to give him the riot act. They were in disbelief and made their voices heard on the matter. Not once did Colins reply, he knew the agent was listening. Waiting for the evidence he needed to keep him locked up. Evidence Colins knew he did not have.

"If I had known about your dealings with Porter, I could have helped you," he said, and once again, Colins did not respond.

There was no evidence, but the business card was enough to get a warrant for his house. If Linda was there, she would be upset, but no one would find anything. Never had he and Porter wrote anything down regarding their meetings, transportation routes, or sales. They were smart, at least in that aspect.

"You dug your own grave…" his captain said and walked away.

The change in patrol was signed by the captain with Colins's influence. There was nothing connecting him to a change in patterns, taking evidence, or letting someone go. But there was something wrong with Linda being gone all this time. He needed to find her, but if Colins left, he would finally have a crime that could be used against him.

"All they got is the card," Porter said as he leaned against the bars, his hat and jacket concealing his facial features.

"I am aware. We were too careful," Colins replied and sat up from the bed.

They both were silent as a few officers walked by. No one gave them a glance. With the agent around, he was cracking down on all aspects of the department. Everyone was on high alert. Porter thrived in chaos, which made it so much easier to be left unseen.

"What is on your mind?" Porter asked.

"I need to find Linda."

"Why? She is a grown woman able to make her own choices."

"She has been with me since she was a child. Never kept secrets, but something is going on she doesn't want me to know about." He paced across the room.

"Again, she is an adult."

"This city will suck you in and leave you vulnerable. It has no mercy for the good ones like Linda. The ones who see this world as good are the ones who usually end up getting hurt. I do not want her to get hurt, Porter. I can't let that happen."

"I need you to think about what you are asking."

"I have. In this cell, all you have is your thoughts."

Porter walked to the lock on the cell, and Colins heard the lock click. No one moved or made a sound when Porter threw in a hat and large jacket. They would get out of here through the front door. The one place no one would be looking and find his niece, to protect her from the world they both helped create. But Colins would give up the fight and his freedom as long as Linda was safe.

CHAPTER THIRTEEN

Linda had not been home for at least a week. It was her little form of rebellion from her uncle, but she did leave a note, didn't she? That she was staying with some friends. Whispers grew about who was responsible for the fires and how the federal agents were in the city. All the whispers created a ghost, one that made everyone afraid to go out at night, including Linda.

"What do you mean he got arrested?" Linda yelled as she looked at Conner, who was walking into the apartment.

"As I said. They picked him up a few days ago, and the charges haven't been disclosed," Conner said and walked deeper into the apartment.

With the boys lying low, he had to make the runs. It was not hard, but it meant less merchandise would get moved between each point. Also, Porter was opening only half of his clubs at half capacity. They could not be caught by the feds, which meant everyone had to be careful.

"Is he okay?" Linda whispered as Conner frowned.

Conner's apartment was a far stretch from her townhouse.

Everyone knew Colins came from money; on a detective's salary, he would not have been able to afford that beautiful place. But here, it was two rooms that she made a home. A miracle that was the woman he loved.

Fresh flowers on the table every day and dinner ready for him when he told her he would come home. It was clean, and the hand-crafted blankets and pillows brought light into this darkened place. It was a home, their home, and when Conner walked over to her, he kissed her long and hard.

"He has friends who will take care of him. He is not alone. Neither are you," Conner replied and wrapped his arms around her.

She was warm where he was cold. His heart would beat out of his chest every time he held her. It was like that the first time he took her hand to help her stand. The flower shop. It was where they first met.

A blooming and beautiful southern belle holding a massive bouquet of flowers. She could not see where she was going and was knocked over by a passing car. Conner saw the whole thing and took her hand to help her up. After that, he could not stop thinking about her.

"You always have a flower hidden in my coat. The boys are starting to tease me about smelling too good," Conner said as Linda laughed.

Flowers were their meet cute. It was their signal. Every day,

Conner would find a flower in a place where he was, a place that no flower should ever be. In return, once he learned what Linda was doing, he did the same. A large bouquet would appear on her balcony, every morning for months. All with bright and beautiful flowers. They were as bright as the happiness Linda made Conner feel every time he saw her.

"I need you to stay in the apartment. I know it isn't ideal, but with your uncle in jail, the agents will come after you for any information to keep him locked up," Conner explained.

"What would I say? I would never hurt my uncle," Linda said, almost offended, but Conner did not let her walk out of his arms.

"I know, sweetheart. They will take your words and make them what they want. You never want to see the inside of a police station, and I will make sure they never touch you," he promised and kissed the top of her head.

"I made dinner. Go get cleaned up," Linda said and kissed Conner once more before finally letting go.

The bathroom was the only other room in the apartment. It was small, too small but it held a shower that when it turned on, Linda knew he was in it. She frowned at the very thought of Conner and touched her stomach. It had been months since she had been with Conner, and it also had been months since she last bled.

Being in this apartment, she could not freely move. When Conner was away, he had a few men outside the apartment to protect her, but there was a way for her to move, to always get the fresh flowers, and that would be the fire escape. Never did she go down, she always went up.

One little hop to the next building and then down its fire escape gave her freedom and answers. The paper to confirm her pregnancy was in her pocket, and she did not know how to tell Conner. Would he be angry with her? They had been careful but not careful enough.

The bread was already cooling on the table, and the stew was simmering on the stove. This was her ideal family. A husband who loved and protected them. A man who would never hurt her. But this city, it was toxic, and they could not stay here. But would Conner be willing to

go away from everything he ever knew?

"I will protect you…no matter what…" Linda whispered to her unborn child, letting out a startled gasp when a loud knock came at the front door.

At first, she thought she was hallucinating. When that knock happened again, the sound of the shower showed Conner did not hear it. When it happened a third time, she walked over to the door and opened it.

It was only a few moments after that knock that Conner got out of the shower and dried himself. There was always a clean pile of clothing waiting for him, a small gesture. The little things Linda always thought of made him smile and feel cared for. But when

Conner walked out of the bathroom, the apartment was empty.

The stew on the stove was bubbling over, and the door was wide open. There was no Linda. His heart was beating out of his chest. It was not with love like before but out of fear. Where was Linda? Who would dare take something that was his? Did they know who he worked for?

—

The smell of fresh flowers hit Linda's nose. It was not emanating from a small bundle on the table, rather from the entire room. Only one place smelled this way, and when she opened her eyes, Linda looked at the flower shop around her.

It was dark; the only light was a single candle on the table in front of her. It was then she realized her arms were tied behind the chair she was sitting on, her legs immobile. When she tried to call out, her voice was muffled. She was defenseless and at the mercy of the person she heard walking around the room.

"Linda Bishop. Boston's own southern belle in the flesh,"

a familiar voice said as Linda tried to scream.

Paul Daniels. That voice was like nails on a chalk board. Everyone knew and hated him, but he had her vulnerable and weak. As Daniels finally showed his face, he was standing on the other side of the table with an evil grin.

"Who would have ever thought you would fall head over heels for Conner McDonald," Daniels said while Linda struggled and screamed.

Daniels only laughed at her struggle, her pain. It took a lot of digging to learn who had caught Conner's heart. That man had shaken every tail Daniels had put on him, but when Colins was arrested, it gave Daniels the opportunity to follow his niece around and find that special something to keep that detective in jail.

He knew she was pregnant. The doctor's office and her whispering to herself about Conner's baby proved. She was Daniels's ticket to Senator Murphy taking him seriously. Everyone needed him, and if the future president was in his back pocket, he would be unstoppable.

"Does Conner know about the baby?" Daniels asked as he knelt in front of Linda.

That sentence stopped her from struggling. The thought of harm coming to her unborn child caused tears to fall down her face. She was in trouble, Linda knew that, but when Daniels raised a match and lit it, all he did was smile.

"I am sorry you had to die like this…so young and full of innocence. You will be the shining example that all good girls should stay away from bad boys. That will get you killed in the very place you first saw him. Goodbye, Linda Bishop," Daniels said and threw the lit match behind her.

Linda screamed and thrashed, once more as smoke filled the room. That smell of flowers was replaced by the smell of smoke. It was the smoke that Daniels walked into and disappeared. She needed to get out of here, needed to survive. She needed to see her beloved once more.

—

"What do you mean Linda is gone?" Porter demanded as he met Conner an hour after she went missing.

"The door was wide open, and dinner was still on the stove. She was taken right out of my own damn apartment. It wasn't someone small…" Conner said as they both turned at the sound of someone screaming.

"Fire!"

The flower shop was already up in flames the moment the two men ran in front of it. The flowers added fuel to the fire, and there was no sound of the alarm bells to indicate help was coming. People were already trying to get inside to see if they could stop it, and Conner and Porter ran forward to help without a second thought.

Linda was unconscious, sitting in that chair, waiting to die. The amount of smoke she had inhaled had made it hard to breathe, but when Betty Tyler started to untie her arms, that sudden movement slowly stirred her awake.

"Linda! Linda!" Betty kept yelling.

The fire was hot, too hot, but Betty untied her arms and went to her legs. The rope was not tied tight, but in Linda's panic, she had tightened them. When Linda was free, she was barely moving.

"You better not be heavy…" Betty mumbled as she slowly leaned Linda into her back and stood.

Having to fend for herself on the streets made Betty strong. The clothing she wore, baggy and barely attached to her body, hid the muscle. She was stronger than she looked but needed to seem weak.

If she were weak, their guard would be down, and if they saw the knives she had on her person, they would not be so easily grounded. Betty needed to hide to stay anonymous from all police raids and questionings. As she carried Linda out of the back, she immediately saw Conner and Porter trying to find a way in.

"Jesus…" Conner muttered as he caught sight of Betty carrying Linda.

The two men immediately were at her side, and Conner took Linda into his arms. She was covered in soot and barely breathing, but when Conner held her close, she stirred.

"The baby…" Linda mumbled before she once again fell unconscious.

"Take her to the hospital. Now!" Porter ordered as Conner did so, without looking to the woman who saved her life.

"We are grateful," Porter said as Betty scoffed.

"Save it. Conner has a weakness, and it was exposed tonight. Either he and his girl must leave town or it will leave you at risk. She kept talking about a baby in her sleep. So, he knocked up a girl? Typical."

"What do you want in order to keep this girl and her baby a secret?" Porter asked, getting straight to business.

"I do not need your money."

"Then what do you want?"

What did she want? Money was something she could always get and a place to spend the night was not hard to find. But what she wanted was freedom. From this life, this city, and to do that, she needed connections.

"You know what I want," Betty said and limped away.

The chaos of the fire hid her departure. Hid the fact that Linda Bishop was in the middle of it and that the real target was Conner McDonald. Secrets. Each fire hid a secret that the police would never find, and the federal agents would only scratch the surface. One needed to live on the streets to understand them, and Betty was the one that everyone needed, even if they would never admit it.

CHAPTER FOURTEEN

"I have had three buildings all in the same block light up like a Christmas tree. All acts were declared an act of arson and the fire marshal said accelerant was used. We need to stop this. Get ahead of this before it gets out of control and we have a riot on our hand," the mayor said with a serious expression as he faced a crowd of concerned

individuals.

For ten days, City Hall had been active. Everyone was trying to solve the unsolvable. Not only did Prohibition cause them a whole bunch of problems but also was the arson something no one needed right now. With Detective Colins in the wind and the federal agents on the streets, it was only a matter of time before it all cracked and fell apart.

"The accelerant was the same at all three businesses. It seems the butcher shop was the only incident that held any casualties," an aide explained.

"Tell me about the first one," the mayor demanded.

"O'Malley Grocery. They immigrated from Ireland thirty years ago. A father and his two sons," another aide explained and flipped a paper as another spoke up.

"The grocery store is legit. There has been no evidence of money laundering or connections to any organized crime. The father is straight, but the sons, on the other hand, were taken in by the sweet smell of money to do things to keep their father's business afloat."

"Tell me of the charges we can bring against them we have actual proof of," the mayor asked.

An aide stood up and walked over to the many boards that covered the walls. Evidence of each arson case, those involved, and the victims were all exposed. Suspected attackers were identified with notes beside their pictures.

"Finnick and Patrick O'Malley have been seen at local known drop sights where two grocery delivery men have no place being. Each brother holds enough body mass and stamina to fight his way out of a situation, which we believe was the case with the abandoned truck found by the local sheriff."

Agent Willard sat in the back. He was in every meeting and always remained quiet in the back of the room. He looked at the information presented before him. He was sent here to clean up the mess that Boston was facing. Looking at the brother's mug shots, he felt that something did not settle right, and he was a man to never stay quiet when something was bothering him.

"Where are they now?" Willard asked.

"Um, after they were in our custody for a few weeks, they were released. We could not bring them back in because we had no evidence to tie them to the truck," the aide explained as Willard stood and approached the boards.

He had been here long enough to see a pattern, to know who was playing the game and who was caught in the crosshairs. One had to have connections in high places to make things happen. For Porter to avoid detection and move so freely meant he had help and with all the evidence to connect Porter to Colins as boys, his disappearance confirmed it.

"Let's not focus on the narrative of the arsons but rather the connection to a man we are all familiar with," Willard said and put the picture of Detective Colins on a clean board.

"Agent Willard," the mayor began, but Willard was done sitting back and letting others tell him what he already knew.

"Detective Benjamin Colins was arrested for being an associate of Porter, also known as Emmet Colins, the foster brother of our dear detective." Willard placed Porter's image next to the detective's.

"What are we looking at?" Senator Murphy asked as he and everyone else was intrigued to know where this was going.

"Ladies and Gentlemen, I give you the masterminds behind the city of Boston. The Colins Brothers," Willard said and then looked through his stack of papers and put up the picture of Linda Bishop next to Benjamin Colins.

"Emmet Colins has no known familial associates besides his brother. No wife, children, or mistress. But Benjamin Colins has a niece who was put under his care when she was young. Linda was from a traditional southern town in Louisiana, so the culture shock and difference made it hard for the child to adjust."

"As a result, and numerous complaints of theft, ill-mannered speaking and judgmental tones…this is my way of not spreading the racial slurs…she caught the eye of one Conner McDonald," the agent explained as he put the picture of Conner underneath the three, other photos.

"Kids are kids. Why did you put Linda up there when the poor child has been missing for over a month?" an aide asked in a judgmental tone.

Willard put up a photograph that was taken only yesterday. He showed the time stamp of Linda leaning up against a sign about a sale at O'Malley's Grocery, the date on the sale starting today. O'Malley only put those signs up the day before and took them down before the sun rose that day. He was a businessman.

"Linda is alive and well. We do not know where she is hiding, but we know who she is hiding with. Witness accounts have placed Linda in the arms of Mr. McDonald, and the romantic public relations confirm they are indeed a couple."

"How did you get all this information?" Senator Murphy asked.

"Emmet Colins, has had competition challenge him throughout the years, but nobody has been able to top Porter's market, production, and reputation. An anonymous tip from a disgruntled runner-up also known as Lawrence Murphy has been very helpful since we picked him up for public intoxication," Willard explained and put up the mugshot of Lawrence.

"And you trust him?" an aide asked.

"Everything Lawrence Murphy gave us has been confirmed by his foster sister Connie Murphy as she came forward to aid in his attempt for a reduced sentence," Willard said as he cleared his throat.

Willard had been there when Lawrence was arrested. He was an angry drunk, spewing nonsense, but when Connie ran out of the apartment to assist him, she was in horrible shape. A busted lip, a newly formed black eye, and her visible skin was all bruised. It was no mistake

she had been beaten but she refused to say by whom.

He had nothing to keep her in the station, but he did convince her to go to the hospital. Willard ordered a few agents to stay close in case the one that hurt her came back. But he had a sneaky suspicion it was Lawrence. The way he looked at her, with a fiery passion and hatred, was a look he saw on abusers all the time. But there was nothing he could do for Connie unless she was willing to come forward.

Agent Willard looked around the room briefly and locked his gaze on Senator Hamilton Murphy. The agent showed no sympathy towards the knowledge a woman was injured. Even after Willard put up the picture of Connie's battered face, his expression was cold.

"Murphy confirmed what we all suspected. Finnick and Patrick O'Malley are the transportation of Porter's product."

"Is that why the grocery store was targeted?" the mayor asked.

"It could be," Willard began and turned to face the group to continue.

"Finnick O'Malley has been openly seen approached by Gretchen Laird, an aide to this very office. Many witnesses state she presented O'Malley with gifts, pastries, and love letters. What makes this romance even sweeter is that Gretchen Laird is the sister of known driver to Porter, Manny Laird." He pointed to their pictures.

That news made a few aides whisper. They all knew that the past few days Gretchen had called out sick.

They all suspected the flu, but seeing her picture up there made

them all suspect it was something more. That mumbling is what Willard wanted; he wanted that doubt to be placed before he continued his presentation.

"The other brother, Patrick O'Malley, has been seen making advances towards college student Cameron Mitchell. She was a victim of the butcher shop fire. Thankfully, she survived but holds visible scars

on both of her legs." Willard placed a picture of Vincent Sullivan next to Cameron.

"And who is this?" the senator asked, trying to hold his expression of seeing the man he loved on that board.

"Vincent Sullivan is an employee at the clothing store that is next to O'Malley Grocery. On numerous occasions, he has been seen in conversation with the brothers and was arrested in the riot after the fire. His encounters are ruled out as more than a coincidence."

When a picture of Betty Tyler went up next, all the men cleared their throats. It was no secret what her occupation was and that many upper-class individuals used her from time to time, but Willard looked to the senator.

"Say it," Senator Murphy said, knowing it was no secret.

"Betty Tyler is a well-known prostitute of the area. In our information gathering, every man in this room has been in her service at one time or another, but we are not here to stop prostitution." He put a picture of Senator Murphy and Paul Daniels next to the picture of Betty.

When Paul went up, people turned to look at him. Like the senator, Paul's expression was cold and unreadable. It seemed Willard had a target on everyone, not only the known suspects they were prepared to take in. When a picture of Sarah Monroe went up, a few people frowned.

"Sarah Monroe has been seen on numerous occasions bringing food, medicine, and clothing to Miss Tyler. These transactions were routine as if they have been doing it for years. But the amount of clothing that leaves both women's hands are in trade. Why would a schoolteacher be trading with a prostitute?"

"The same goes for Senator Hamilton Murphy and Secretary

Paul Daniels. These two men have also been seen exchanging items with Miss Betty Tyler routinely. There are services who reached out to Miss Tyler to give her assistance, but she refused on all counts. So, why does she accept help from these three individuals? One word…information," Willard said as he took a step away from the board.

Sixteen individuals had their pictures on that wall. All with page after page of information connected to each other. Willard kept adding evidence until it took up three boards and then he grabbed a folder from the floor and dropped it on the middle of the table.

"As of right now, I am declaring war. In thirty days, we will bring these sixteen individuals in for questioning, and if they cannot be found, we will assume that they are guilty and a manhunt will begin," Willard said as his eyes met the senator, who still had no expression on his face.

That meeting gave every patrol officer a face to look for. Senator Hamilton and Paul Daniels were now under house arrest until further investigation. Both men were silent; even when reporters reached out for their statements, they did not say a word. Silence was key because the first one amongst the group who talked would bring the entire empire down with them.

CHAPTER FIFTEEN

"You are brooding," Porter said to his brother as Detective Colins smashed the peanut on the countertop with his fist.

"I am fine," he replied and popped the peanut into his mouth.

"She has every right to love whomever she wants," Porter added as Colins hit another peanut hard on the counter.

When he walked out of that prison and out of the police station, he knew he could not go back. He was a criminal. His townhouse was ceased, and all his assets were frozen. At this moment, Colins did not care. All he cared about was protecting his brother and his niece, but in hearing the news of her pregnancy and by whom, he was anything but thrilled.

"He knocked her up!" Colins snapped.

"Conner is making it right by marrying her. I can't lose him; you know that."

"I won't kill him…maybe hurt him a little bit." He punched the counter, not caring if he had a peanut under his fist or not.

"Regardless of the pain you are feeling, now isn't the time. We have bigger problems than this little family drama."

When the war on crime was started, it meant more law

enforcement would be added to the already growing roster. More manpower from out of state with fresh eyes and an ambition to make a name for themselves. This is how people got killed, but it also got the job done. They were in trouble; they both knew it.

"I do not know when the crackdown will begin. I lost all of my intel by walking out of that cell," Colins reminded Porter as the door opened and Patrick O'Malley walked in.

Both men looked over at Patrick, who appeared as depressed and upset as Colins felt. Poor kid. He and his brother learned recently that their father was sick, and they could not be at his side. If they left the protection Porter was providing, their father could be charged with conspiracy to commit a crime and harboring a fugitive. They did not want that for him.

Their father had no backup plan if one of the boys could not run the store in his absence. Porter promised the shop and the apartment would be protected, but to pay their father's medical bills, both brothers needed to work for Porter full time.

"He is stable. No news is good news. The doctors are working hard to fight the infection in his lungs, and he is too stubborn to die before yelling at the two of you for being stupid," Porter explained.

"We need to see him," Patrick begged for the first time in his entire life.

"Any movement day or night holds too much of a risk," Colins said while Patrick looked to the ground.

"Cheer up, kid. This won't last forever," Porter said, and Patrick nodded.

"I know. I wish I could help is all," Patrick added, but Porter was already distracted by the notebook on the table.

Having to reorganize, redistribute, and pay the salaries was hitting the funds he had saved up. Those savings were there in case they were frozen in place. The little war on crime tantrums never lasted long; they got one good hit and then backed off. If all of Porter's players stayed hidden, they would be fine.

"What are you thinking?" Colins asked.

"We stay hidden…wait till this blows over." Patrick threw a chair in hearing that answer from Porter.

Doing nothing to him was the same as giving up, but Porter was the boss. Everyone trusted him to have their best interest at heart, but it was hard. Being in charge made him doubt everything, including himself.

—

"I am scared," Linda whispered as she and Conner remained safe in a room.

Porter's entire estate was underground. The wars fought overseas had everyone building bunkers out of fear of bombs falling from the sky. Porter was no different, but he made this massive estate large enough for twenty people, his key players. The ones he needed to be kept close. He had to keep an eye on them, so they were trapped right where he wanted them.

"I know," Conner replied and held her close.

One of his hands rested behind her head and the other was on her stomach. When he learned of his child growing inside her, he became even more protective of Linda. Never was she allowed to go out alone,

not anymore. Being taken from him once was enough to have the

fear of losing her forever. A fear he will never feel again.

"He couldn't even look at me. My uncle hates me," Linda said, fighting back the tears.

"He doesn't hate you. It is your poor choice in men he hates."

There was no making the mood lighter. They were stuck here in this underground bunker for an unknown amount of time. It was stressful on everyone, but Linda felt like this was all her fault. That her deception caused all of this to fall apart.

—

Porter paced back and forth in his office, knowing full well a sizeable amount of people relied on him. He did not want to be a martyr. His goal was to make a comfortable life for himself and his brother. Those under his employment would get his protection. But now, so many people were looking to him for answers, ones he did not know if he could ever give.

"Damn it…" Porter muttered.

He had a nagging headache from the lack of sleep. Too many variables made it nearly impossible for him to do this alone. Pride would not only get him killed but also risk everyone in this bunker. Which meant he needed outside help.

CHAPTER SIXTEEN

They could not do this alone. A handful of people could not change the world, but enough would raise a voice, one that many would be forced to listen to. That voice was what he needed, and as Porter put his feet on the familiar cobblestone of the quiet Boston streets, he slowly went from store to store, proposing an idea, a plan that everyone immediately agreed to.

"We need to take our city back. These agents will bleed us dry until there is nothing left," Porter said to the owner of the clothing store as Vincent listened.

Vincent had never wanted to draw any attention to himself. To openly love another, was a death sentence. When Porter walked out of the owner's office, Vincent was startled and fell backwards, drawing their attention.

"Vincent will do whatever you need him to do. He was already arrested with the O'Malley brothers, so his reputation is in favor with the Irish," the owner said as Porter nodded before walking away.

Vincent needed to live his life in secret, and to do that, he had to be invisible. His clothing was always in neutral tones, which made it easier to blend into the background. He was not overly tall or big, so weaving in and out of the crowds was easy to do.

He needed to see him. There was nothing more needed now than to be held, to be loved by someone who did not look at him as something not worth their time. The sewers were how Vincent got around. It held a bad smell, but it got him right into the back yard of a well-known man. The manhole cover was left unscrewed for this very reason.

—

Senator Murphy was in his study, a cigar in one hand and a paper in the other. This whole house arrest was nonsense, but a federal agent had a level of pull that he did not have. No one believed the rubbish that was spoken at that meeting, but it held enough doubt to continue an investigation into him.

He did not move when he heard the back door open because it was always locked. Only one man had a key to it and Murphy let out a sigh of content when he heard those footsteps go up the stairs. Murphy had told Vincent time and time again he did not need to take a shower, but Vincent was adamant to get the smell of the outside off his skin before they touched.

"I missed you," Vincent said softly sometime later, when he found Hamilton in the same spot, looking out a window.

Murphy did not reply; he closed his eyes when he felt Vincent's hands on his shoulders. Slowly those hands wrapped around him and pulled him close. Vincent was so much smaller than him, but they fit so perfectly together. Silence. It followed them only for a

moment. But as Vincent kissed his neck, Murphy reached up and touched his face.

"Are you safe?" Murphy asked as Vincent slowly let go, only to walk around the chair to now stand before him.

The window looked out to the city below and this was not the first time the two of them had been in front of it. It was almost a challenge, a dare to have anyone look in and see what they were doing. Vincent slowly leaned forward, putting his knee in-between Murphy's legs as he gently grabbed his tie.

"I am safe now that I am with you," Vincent replied and pulled him in for a kiss.

They loved each other. Every bit of what they had was true. A kiss. A night. That is all they could ever have, but the senator demanded to see him, needed to see him. His touch broke that cold heart, and it started to beat. Like he needed him to breathe.

"Vincent," Hamilton whispered when he felt his shirt unbutton.

Rather than speak, Vincent kissed him again. No number of words can make the fear of the unknown disappear. All either man needed right now was to feel. To feel the one they loved and make sure their hellish life was a distant memory.

—

They talked about everything, and Vincent never told a soul. The senator needed someone to hear his story, the true story, and when the topic of his foster siblings came up, Vincent listened. There was only one woman in the senator's life that he cared about, in his own twisted way.

"I can't help her...She loves him too much," Hamilton said as Vincent slowly raised his head on the bed they were lying in.

Everyone was whispering about her bruises, her marks. They knew someone was hurting her. Hamilton knew it was Lawrence. He wanted to kill that bastard but could not; it would only add fuel to the fire that was slowly growing around him.

"Love can make someone blind, or it can awaken the fire that has cursed them their entire life," Vincent replied and touched the hair on Murphy's chest.

Senator Murphy growled at the thought of someone hurting what he cared about most, and he suddenly moved Vincent as close as possible. He needed to taste him again. Customs be damned, this was right, and this feeling was love. He did not care what others thought, and Murphy wanted, no begged, someone to see what he was doing to this man because if he was going to lose everything, he wanted at least to be with someone who knew all of him.

CHAPTER SEVENTEEN

One month. That was how long everyone had been silent. How long the entire city was walking on eggshells as Willard proceeded with his investigation. It was nonstop. Every night the agents would patrol the streets, go door to door, demanding information about Porter and his gang, but no one would talk.

The entire community was protecting him, protecting their own. Willard understood the loyalty, but as he walked in the middle of the quiet night, he knew something needed to happen. They were at a standstill; something needed to push one side to attack the other. Never had Willard been known for being a dirty agent, but he stopped right in the middle of the street and looked at the closed grocery store.

The sound of children in the distance showed that many were now home and that Willard was free to do what was needed to be done. Each of these businesses was Irish-owned in an Irish neighborhood.

They protected their own. Many people on occasion accused him of betraying his blood because of the color of his hair, the freckles on his face, and the accent in his voice. It was what he was born with, how he talked before his family left Ireland when he was a teenager.

Willard missed home. He hated the city, but that was where the jobs were. Where both of his parents needed to be to make enough money for their brew. But the alcohol, the substance that was found, destroyed his family. Never again would he see another family destroyed, so when he looked to the clothing store, he frowned.

Something needed to happen for the fuse to be lit, and as young Vincent Sullivan walked out of the store, Willard raised his service pistol. The quiet ones were usually the ones that were well-connected. Willard's face was hidden behind his hat and coat, but as he pulled the trigger, he was still facing Vincent.

It echoed in the quiet night, and a loud pop caused the residence in the surrounding apartment to awaken and find their way to the body. Vincent Sullivan had a secret, and up until yesterday, no one knew that secret.

Right before Lawrence Murphy was sentenced to life without parole, he told the world that Patrick O'Malley was blackmailing Senator Hamilton Murphy. The court laughed it off because Senator Murphy had nothing in his financial records of him withdrawing large amounts of cash, but when he said that he was having an affair with Vincent Sullivan, Willard knew exactly what had to happen to make this war begin.

"Was that a gunshot?" someone screamed.

Vincent slowly brought a hand to his stomach where it started to hurt. When he looked down to his hand, he saw red. Slowly, his legs gave out as he fell to the ground. Another scream filled the air the

moment they saw Vincent, and others started to gather around him.

"Vincent has been shot!" someone yelled.

A few people saw a man walking away, a man that was wearing a black rain jacket from the local police department. Vincent tried to breathe, but it hurt, too much to bear.

"Is he breathing?" someone asked

"Easy son, we will get you to the hospital," a man said, but Vincent grabbed onto his arm tightly.

Blood was slowly seeping from his mouth, so when he tried to talk, it came out as a gurgle. He was dying. He knew he was, and Vincent did not want to be here, in the arms of a man that he didn't know. No, he wanted his senator, but when he took one more deep breath, no more breaths followed.

—

That morning, the entire city woke up to the news of an Irish boy being shot. A man that never harmed anyone in his entire life. Vincent now lay dead, in the middle of a room filled with metal and chemicals. His body was opened, and the bullet was removed. It did not take long for the mortician to declare the cause of death a single bullet to the abdomen, one that pierced his liver and entered his intestine.

Vincent drowned in his own blood and now lay cold and alone. When the news made its way to the senator, he yelled out a scream that everyone could hear. One of grief, sorrow, and pain. Loud bangs and crashes caused the patrolmen to break into his house and restrain him.

Senator Hamilton Murphy was covered in tears, bloodied from broken glass and dust. He was destroying everything he touched out of grief, and that made the connection of Vincent and himself known. That was enough for City Hall to call an emergency meeting with all law

enforcement because the bullet was from one of their revolvers.

"This city is on the brink of madness!" the mayor yelled

while hundreds of uniformed officers stood there, tired from the lack of sleep and fear of what was about to happen.

"It has been confirmed that the bullet that killed Vincent Sullivan was from a service pistol," an aide explained.

"It can't be proven. All they saw was a man in a hat and jacket. That could be anyone!" an officer yelled.

"People are losing faith in our ability to keep them safe. Which is making our investigation Difficult," a detective said. Willard did not move when an agent leaned over to whisper to him.

"The senator was taken into custody. The news of the man's death resulted as expected." Willard nodded.

"They have blocked entrances to the streets. Some have full-on barricades!" an officer shouted, and the mayor sighed.

This was getting out of hand. The screaming and hollering were getting them nowhere. The politicians demanded action, but law enforcement could not keep up. Willard snuck out of the room easily and met up with his agents in a secret room to discuss what they were going to do.

"The third and fourth grids are now completely blocked from assistance," an agent reported.

"Water and electricity?" Willard asked.

"Off. If they do not willingly comply, they will not be given the services the city provides. They will not give up Porters gang, no matter what we do," one informed.

"Keep the first two grids open and make sure the mayor doesn't see the last two. We know he is in there; all we need to do is get him to come out," Willard said as his team nodded.

They were trying to draw out Porter at the risk of the people who were protecting him. After the shooting, no one opened their doors to the police or talked with them. Before the death of Vincent, people would give minimum information, enough so they would not suspect them. But that one bullet changed everything.

—

"Vincent was innocent!" Conner yelled as he looked to Porter who was in the back of the schoolhouse.

This was bigger than all of them. It was not about the Eighteenth Amendment and Prohibition. All the Irish were being targeted, shaken down, and accused of crimes they did not commit. The agents were ruthless, separating families and turning off electricity and water. This was madness, illegal, but no one was going to stop them.

"He hasn't been the first innocent to have lost his life," Sarah said, and everyone in the room fell silent.

"They arrested the senator. They learned he was more than friends with Vincent," Finnick said as Patrick scoffed at the news he already knew.

"What are we to do? We fled Ireland to get away from this kind of brutality," someone said in the crowd.

He did not want it to have to come to violence. There was a time when violence repulsed him, but there were guns aligned on the walls, more and more being collected. The entire block was waiting for a fight, the one that the law enforcement would start by breaking down their door and demanding answers.

"I say we fight them!" someone yelled as many agreed.

Porter would not go into the hands of the law alive. He would have to be dead, cold, and hardened to get anywhere near a jail cell.

He was ready to die, but Conner looked antsy.

 He had a child on the way and a woman he loved. Something had changed in the man; he had become too cautious. That cautiousness could lead to an irreversible mistake.

"I want you on the train tomorrow, Conner," Porter said, and everyone in the room looked over to Conner, confused by what was happening.

"What the hell is that supposed to mean?" Conner spat.

"Don't be stupid. You have a kid on the way, and Linda cannot get involved in this."

"You're taking this personally!" Connor yelled, but this time, Porter was louder.

"Of course I am taking this goddamn personally. Linda may not be my niece by blood, but her uncle is my brother by circumstance. That is my family, which makes you a part of this. You, Conner McDonald, will be on that train, or I will chain you to it myself!" The entire room watched the two of them.

This was really going to happen. Everyone was arming themselves for a fight. Guns would be blazing, and people would be dying. A party for all those who were rooting for the number of souls that would be collected by the end of the night...

THE FINAL CHAPTER

"We have a sighting of Emmet Colins, also known as Porter!" an agent yelled as he ran into Willard's office.

A large map rested on the table in front of Agent Willard. Markings covered it with potential sightings of Porter and his associates. They tried every angle to flush him out, even killing one of his own, but it did not work. Willard made his move; now he had to wait for Porter to make his.

"Where?" Willard demanded, still not moving because every response he had gotten for that very question had resulted in disappointment.

"A café off of main," the agent said.

Willard held up a finger to silence him. Porter wasn't this stupid; he would not be caught out in the open. Why would he be at a café? This whole situation did not make any sense.

"What is the source?" he asked.

"Solid. The man is sitting at the table outside the café," the agent replied, and Willard grabbed his coat, out the door before another word could be spoken.

—

Porter was there, sitting at the table and drinking a beer. Prohibition meant nothing when his entire world was destroyed. His calm, comfortable life was now at risk, and he could not have that.

His people were being treated like rats, needing to be exterminated because no one felt like they had a reason to belong. He would not stand for it, and as he expected, the agent in charge appeared. Rather than come over guns blazing, the man sat down across from him and put his hat on the table.

"Heard you were looking for me," Porter said as Willard looked at the beer and frowned.

"You have been a hard man to find, Mr. Colins." When Porter heard the accent, he laughed.

"The rumor about you being an Irishman is true, yet you turn against your own kind. Explain that to me," Porter said, taking another sip of the one thing the world hated more than him right now.

"Even though we all came from the same country, it doesn't make us equal. That beer in your hand cost many families their happiness."

"So, that is your story. Mom and Pop piss it all away for the liquid glory, and you take all your anger out on everyone else.

Well, news flash, young one, life is full of pitfalls and drama. How you learn from them will mold you into the man you will become."

"You act like you know me."

"I know the type. Young, ambitious, trying to change the world, but you're going at it on the wrong side."

"And why is that?"

"I am a businessman; my main concern is making sure my customers are satisfied. I am that way in life as well. Those who work for me came to me with a problem. Some of those problems are money-related, but others are a lack of hope or a sense of peace. There is a need in this world, one to make life worth living and demanding people to follow rules so blindly is not the way for them to live."

"Even when it is in their best interest?"

"Especially when it is in their best interest. No one will know what is best for someone else." Porter slowly stood.

Porter was known to be calculated and calm under pressure. That was how he was appearing here today, which worried Willard. But, as the man took his beer and finished it off, he threw the bottle on the ground and pointed to the end of the street.

There stood four teams, over one hundred individuals who were under Willard's rule. Porter knew that this was going to be a situation where they had to fight it out, but an old-fashioned standoff interested him. Porter took a few steps back as he slowly raised his hands, keeping his eyes on Willard the entire time.

"What is it going to take Mr. Colins, for you to see the error of your ways?" Willard called out.

"If you see my actions as wrong, there is no hope you will see the reasons behind what I do. If you want me so bad, Agent Willard, come and get me," he said and disappeared down an alley.

There was no way around this. This meeting was to draw the target out, to make him see that no one was backing down.

A standoff.

A fight. A need to be validated. Any number of reasons brought everyone to the side they chose, but to Porter, it was personal.

"What is the plan?" Patrick asked Porter.

The boss walked down the alley with haste, and Finnick handed a Tommy gun. The reason for Porter showing himself was to bring the enemy to him. No one was going to fight in unfamiliar territory, and if they were to die, it would be on their own soil.

"We will not shoot first. I do not need the papers to say we shot first," Porter demanded and turned quickly.

There was only one way into the city, and there only needed to be one leader. Benjamin, his brother, the former Detective Colins, wanted to fight, but Porter needed someone he could trust to guide everyone to safety. He did not need to soil his hands with the blood that was about to be spilled. When the brothers said their goodbyes, Porter felt like it would be the last time he would see him.

He didn't make it a step before he bumped into Sarah, and she fell backwards. She had a bag filled with medical supplies that spilled around her feet. Everyone was fighting in their own way. The ones who did not have a gun in their hand were tucked away in a safe place. They could not leave the city. Agent Willard made sure of that, but they were hidden in a place that they would never be found.

"We need everyone on alert!" Porter yelled, helping Sarah up before walking around her.

The distant sounds of gunfire showed that the battle had begun. They were fighting for their freedom to choose, to live, and to be the people they wanted to be. No more rules, no more segregation to a certain part of the city; they deserved a chance at happiness, and this was their chance to get it.

"I want the two of you at my back," Porter ordered to the O'Malley brothers.

Porter's mind was reviewing the plan and each step they were to take to come out of this alive. But his thought process was cut short when he saw Conner. That man was supposed to be on a train with Linda, who was standing at his side. Conner had a rifle in his hand and a smirk on his face. The man never did listen.

"Before you yell at me, the Mrs. wanted to fight. What she says goes…" Conner said as Linda only laughed.

"This is not what we agreed on," Porter said while Linda took a step forward.

"You have no right to make choices for my family. We are staying. We will fight for our home like everyone else," she said, and Porter could not help but smile in approval.

There was a talk, a long talk about what would happen now that there was a baby. Porter gave them a choice, to go back to Louisiana or any city in America they wanted, but by seeing them here, Porter knew their choice was made. Porter did not know if he should be proud of the kid for not abandoning him or mad that he was not taking care of himself, but he was here now, one more person to protect this community.

"Linda, take cover, keep your head down. Conner, let's do this," Porter said and kept moving forward.

There was no time to think, to breathe. Finnick grabbed Porter as a bullet grazed the brick opening of the alley. It was the Wild West out there, and as the bullets flew, Porter frowned. He needed to get out there, but Willard was keeping him in the alleys. They wanted Porter dead, he knew this, but because of that, he had to be extra careful.

—

"He needs to be in a coffin, looking picture-perfect by sundown!" Willard yelled with a pistol in his hand.

No one wanted to see this part. The struggle, the fight. The politicians all wanted change, but how it was enforced was all hush-hush. When Willard turned to fire, he was pointing the weapon right in Daniels's face.

"You want to keep them alive," Daniels said.

"What the fuck are you doing here?" Willard demanded.

"Making sure you do not mess this up. We need Porter alive to make a statement that this city cannot be run by crime."

With the gun still pointed at Daniels's face, Willard screamed and pulled the trigger. Daniels. Paul fucking Daniels. It was he, the man that started this all. In Willard's search, he learned all about the man that lurked in the shadows, and no one wanted to see. The man that had his hand in every death in this city.

The arson cases, every one of them was linked back to him. Betty Tyler. She knew everything and everyone, and when Willard offered her a train ticket anywhere in the country, the woman spilled her guts. That was all it took, for someone to listen, to help her find a better life. She never wanted to be here but had no choice. Not until Willard gave her one.

Willard learned how Gretchen Laird was mad at Finnick O'Malley for flirting with Cameron Mitchell. That anger went to her brother, Manny Laird, who got Paul Daniels involved. The butcher shop was a lack of information on the O'Malley brothers, and the flower shop, he was willing to kill an innocent woman because of her family's relation. This man had to be stopped.

"It should have hurt…" Willard muttered and jumped over Daniels's lifeless body before running into the alleys.

"Sir," one of his agents said as Willard dodged right to avoid a bullet.

"Have we made any progress?" Willard demanded.

"No sir, there are too many unknown assailants, and they are coming at us from all directions."

People were shooting from the street level and from their homes. It was not only Porter's gang that was firing at them but also everyone. There was a kill order on anyone who raised arms against the federal agents, but Willard didn't expect it to be everyone.

—

"These dumb asses are trapped!" Patrick yelled to his brother with a smile.

"Don't get too cocky; there could be more of them," Finnick replied and took cover down an alleyway with his brother.

Endless. The debris, vandalism, and bodies seemed to be endless. At every turn there was chaos. As Patrick turned to follow Finnick, he felt something sharp, painful hit his chest. It took him a moment to register that something was happening, and as he fell to the floor, Finnick was immediately at his side.

"What the hell, Patty?" Finnick muttered to his brother, who was not yet in shock.

"I, um… don't know what happened," Patrick said.

Patrick went to move, but the pain that radiated all over his body caused him to grunt. They needed help, but there were endless people around. Finnick knew he could not trust anyone, but he grabbed Sarah as she ran by. Rather than saying a word, Sarah looked to

Patrick and only nodded, running back from where she came, looking for help.

"You will be all right, Brother. Hang in there," Finnick said as Porter arrived, and they both lifted him up.

"You're a heavy fucker…" Porter mumbled and dropped his pistol to aid his friend.

The fighting continued around them. It did not stop because a few people were running to the one safe place they knew. Each business was closed, and those who could not fight were in hiding. This was not going to stop; the sound of gunfire lasted well into the night. The moment the group entered the O'Malley apartment, our story comes full circle. It was a place where two brothers would never leave the other, no matter where they went or how much danger surrounded them.

Broken glass. The sound of glass shattering was slowly followed by smoke. Like the first fire, it was starting once more. But this time, Finnick did not have the energy to fight. What was left to fight for?

Patrick. His hand was getting cold as his chest no longer rose up and down. Together. They were together always, and when Finnick smelled smoke, he held onto his brother's hands, fighting back the tears.

Their father was now comfortable in the hospital. They were able to meet him before this all had started. Finnick was content in knowing that there would be no tomorrow for him. As the fire rose from the store to the apartment, Finnick closed his eyes and endured it; he would be with his brother, even in death.

—

"Fire!" someone yelled from the outside, but it was not only the O'Malley store that was engulfed.

"Has anyone seen Porter?" Conner yelled as he held Linda close and watched the flower shop once again become ablaze.

"There is no time. Take your woman and run," someone said as Conner looked to Linda and kissed her hand.

They were not the only ones who dropped their arms. With Porter missing, last seen helping the O'Malley brothers, everyone looked to Colins. It was quickly discovered that in his attempt to help a group of school children escape, he was shot and killed. The morale and the need to fight fading.

"Where is Agent Willard?" an agent called out.

On the other side, the agents had not heard from Willard. He was the one who found Colins and happily put a bullet into his head. He saw him as a traitor, a disgrace to the very thing he represented. When Willard took a short cut through the alleys to report back, he vanished. Both groups were without their leaders.

Finnick and Patrick O'Malley. Vincent Sullivan. Detective Benjamin Colins. Paul Daniels. They were now confirmed as deceased. Gretchen Laird. Linda Bishop. Conner McDonald. Cameron Mitchell. They all hid amongst the chaos, finding refuge and praying that they would survive the night. Fear existed. It didn't matter if they were smelling the smoke or watching it from afar; everything everyone knew was falling apart.

Betty Tyler. She found Manny Laird at the train station, that coward was running away before the fight had even started. This wasn't the first time she took a life and gladly sunk her blade into the man who had treated her so poorly. Manny would not leave Boston, and the last thing he saw before he died was a woman who was finally free.

That fire consumed the whole neighborhood, with no way to stop it. It hid the bodies filled with bullet holes and the ones that were

taken under a disguise of a riot. It was this night the people sought their revenge, took their anger, and started their new life with black marks on their souls.

Amongst those bodies were three important people, ones that started their lives together. The Murphy siblings; Connie, Lawrence, and Hamilton. The senator had nothing else to live for;

he found Lawrence in the same jail cell he was being detained, and rather than kill him there, he brought him to the fight. There, he had Connie waiting for him. She would watch, as Hamilton killed their brother, to see the abuser she claimed to love die slowly for the pain he had caused her.

But the fire spread too quickly and consumed them all before anyone could escape. Two men lay on a balcony, overlooking the chaos down below. Their bodies were lifeless. No bullets touched them, but their eyes were white, vacant, and their skin was sunken in as if something precious were taken out. They would not have died otherwise. Those two were too stubborn to die on their own.

Sitting on that balcony in an elegant long black ballroom gown was one woman who had nothing but a smile on her face. A fresh batch of souls for a good night's work would make anyone happy. It was the sweet taste of whisky that passed her ruby lips that made tonight so much sweeter. It made it even better when it was illegal.

That face, everyone knew that face, and when Sarah Monroe looked from the bodies at her side to the fire before her, that smile grew wider. As she investigated the fire, Sarah thought about how it came to this. How she wiggled her way into the community with her volunteer work and slowly got the attention of Porter. He was a man of action, but numbers were his weakness. Everyone had a weakness, and when Sarah showed her loyalty, it was easy to climb up the ladder and gain access to everyone.

A little whisper. That is all anyone needed to be influenced to do her business. A simple conversation could turn violent, a simple cough could turn deadly, and a confused agent with good intentions found a rage inside him he didn't know. It was too easy for her to resist.

As she looked into the fire, Sarah glanced up with those dark eyes and looked right into yours, the readers. She entrapped you and gave a little chuckle at how it all came down to this. How one woman, created out of nothing and put in the middle of it all could start so much chaos. A question that almost seemed...unnatural...

"Dear Reader, did you know it was me?"

The End

S. G. Blinn is an award-winning author that has been writing since she was in grade school. With an education in Media Arts and Digital Design, she brought to life a world that was trapped in her imagination. She designed the book cover for *A Drink With Death* that won the AWAOA Best Book Cover Award 2022. She also won the AWAOA Spirit Award 2022.

She currently resides in New England dreaming up another series of troubled souls that need saving.

Want to stay in touch?

www.sgblinn.com

Made in the USA
Middletown, DE
12 January 2023